the good oak

western literature series

the good oak

MARTIN ETCHART

UNIVERSITY OF NEVADA PRESS / RENO & LAS VEGAS

Mil esker aunties Noeline and Arlette for the help with my Euskara

Western Literature Series

University of Nevada Press, Reno, Nevada 89557 USA

Manufactured in the United States of America

Design by Carrie House

Library of Congress Cataloging-in-Publication Data

Etchart, Martin, 1960–

The good oak / Martin Etchart.

p. cm. — (Western literature series)

ISBN 0-87417-602-6 (pbk. : alk. paper)

1. Grandparent and child—Fiction. 2. Basque Americans—Fiction. 3. Single fathers—Fiction. 4. Sheep herding—Fiction. 5. Immigrants—Fiction. 6. Teenage boys—Fiction. 7. Shepherds—Fiction. 8. Widowers—Fiction.

I. Title. II. Series.

PS3605.T38G66 2005

813'.6—dc22 2004006604

The paper used in this book meets the requirements of American National Standard for Information Sciences—Permanence of Paper for Printed Library Materials, ANSI Z.48-1984. Binding materials were selected for strength and durability.

FIRST PRINTING

14 13 12 11 10 09 08 07 06 05

5 4 3 2 1

Ene aitarenako | for my father

one | bagno

On Sunday, May 6, 1973, I turned thirteen and my world changed. Only not in the way I thought it would.

Up until then, the fact that my dad's parents came from Urepel, France, on a boat from the Basque Country was something I didn't share with my friends. That and how we ate leg of lamb for dinner as often as most other families ate meat loaf, or that instead of having an uncle I had an *oxea* who castrated lambs with his teeth, and a grandpa who didn't live in a retirement community but was a shepherd and spoke a language that sounded like it didn't have either punctuation or vowels.

I knew my family was Basque. I knew my family was different from the families of the kids I went to school with. And I knew that being different wasn't necessarily good. So I kept my family a secret. I figured what the other kids didn't know couldn't hurt me.

So when I woke up that spring morning, I wasn't thinking about anything having to do with being Basque. Changes were what concerned me. The first thing I did was check under my arms for hair. Puberty, I was certain, had arrived some time between 11:59 and midnight. I squinted as I searched for peach fuzz, like Rich Krawski, who had turned thirteen two months earlier, had under his arms. But in the morning light my armpits remained smooth. I ran my fingers over the skin, just to make sure. Nothing. Not giving up, I looked inside my pajama bottoms. There I thought I saw a hair popping up through the white skin, but it turned out to be a piece of bed lint that stuck to my fingertip when I touched it.

Still, I was thirteen. A teenager, even if my body hadn't quite figured that out yet. And hair or no hair, I felt dangerous. While there were still lots of things in the world I didn't know, I awoke that morning confident, unaware that I didn't know them. One of those things was how a bunch of squatty animals covered in dreadlocks could ruin a day that I owned. I soon found out that no one can own a day, but lots of people can take it over. The first to do so was my grandpa.

"He's not coming, is he?" I said when Dad told me we needed to make a quick stop by Grandpa's farm on our way to Phoenix's new amusement park, Legend City.

"Now, then, don't worry," Dad said as he turned onto Camelback Road and headed west. "I just have to get this whole sheep thing sorted out."

Sheep were not what I wanted to talk about on my birthday.

"Rich told me Legend City is way better than Disneyland. No stupid mouse."

"They were just sheep, for God's sake," Dad said as the city's houses were replaced by fields of cotton.

"Let's go on the roller coaster like fifty times."

Dad nodded. "Yeah, fifty."

"And eat tons of cotton candy."

"Sure, candy," Dad said, then added, "Just so you know, I sold Grandpa's sheep."

"All of them?"

"There were only thirty-two left," Dad said.

"Good. They smelled," I said. "Can we stay until it gets dark? I want to ride the Ferris wheel at night."

Dad smiled. "Now, then, how old are you again?"

"Dad . . ."

"Ten? Eleven?"

"You know," I said. "I'm thirteen."

"That's impossible," Dad said. "You sure you're that old?"

"Positive."

Dad laughed and ran a hand through my hair.

"You're getting so big."

"I can touch the basketball rim at school."

"That comes from your mother," Dad said, and then fell silent.

"Was Mom tall?"

"Mmm-hmm," Dad said. "Now, then, where are we going again?"

"Legend City," I said.

"Yes, we are," Dad said.

I grinned, because while going to the amusement park was cool, what made it even cooler was that Dad was going with me. Hanging out together was something we didn't get to do much because of his job. He was the western regional manager for John Deere and traveled out of state a lot, including most weekends, to sell tractors. When Dad went out of town, our next-door neighbor, Mrs. Smith, stayed with me. Mrs. Smith was all right, if you liked hundred-year-old women who smelled like tuna.

When we got to the farm, Grandpa came running across the dirt driveway. Chickens darted between his feet.

"*Zer egin duzu?*" he yelled. "How have you done?"

Grandpa hopped up and down like the ground was on fire.

"Calm down, Dad," my dad said.

"Yeah, cool it, Grandpa," I added.

"Matt, be quiet," Dad said.

"But Legend City ope—"

"Not now, Matt," Dad said.

"*Orai ez du deus ez,*" Grandpa said. "Now we no have nothing."

Grandpa's "we" made me look around for Oxea, Grandpa's brother, and his two worthless dogs, Atarrabi and Mikelats. I was surprised the dogs and Oxea hadn't come running up with Grandpa. The four of them usually traveled in a pack. But Oxea and the dogs were nowhere in sight. Grandpa was on his own.

"*Zu ez zira ene semea,*" he said. "You no my son."

"Now, then, Dad, don't talk like that," Dad said.

Grandpa threw his hands into the air, and dust rose like smoke from the sleeves of his black coat, the coat he wore no matter what the temperature.

"*Horik eneak dira, eta nahi ditut gileat,*" Grandpa said. "They mine, and I want back."

"It's too late," Dad said, and I tilted my head to look at his wristwatch. He was right. Ten precious minutes had already slipped by. If I didn't do something, Legend City was going to open without me. So I stepped between Grandpa and Dad and waved my hand in front of Dad's face.

"We've got to go."

"Matt." Dad pushed my hand down. "Don't interrupt."

I wanted to remind Dad that it was my birthday, but if I

did that, Grandpa would ask how come we weren't spending the day on the farm with him and Oxea? And how come Dad sold the sheep Grandpa was going to give me for a present? That tradition started the year before when instead of getting the tricked-out Schwinn bike I wanted, Grandpa gave me a sheep for my birthday. The sheep was skinny, with big ears and poop stuck to the wool on its rear. To get even, at Christmas I gave the sheep back to Grandpa. But he liked it and said, "I give you two sheeps next year birthday. *Baina* we both get one."

Right then I couldn't risk getting Grandpa going off on that. There wasn't time. So instead I said, "But what about Legend City?"

"Not now," Dad said.

"This stinks."

"Sure, no, stinks," Grandpa said.

"You don't even know what I'm talking about."

I kicked the ground. Anger swelled in my chest, just like it had the week before when I told my teacher, Ms. Helm, that my dad would miss another parent-teacher conference because of an out-of-town meeting. All the other kids' parents would be there. But not my one parent. No, he had tractors to sell. So I stole the matches Rick had hidden in his desk, and in the boys' bathroom I stuffed the trash can full of paper towels. Then I struck a match and dropped it in. The smoke stung my eyes as I watched the paper turn black. The flames grew. My face beaded with sweat. I grabbed another handful of towels to feed into the fire. Then, as I was adding the paper to the fire, I saw her. There, in the flames. A woman. Watching me. I leaned closer. Her hair twisted in curls of yellow and orange; her eyes were dark coals at the center of the blaze. What was she doing in my fire? Heat cupped my face as the woman's lips moved, whispering to me in quick words I couldn't quite make out. Who was she? I opened my mouth to ask her, and when I did both my words and the anger in me were pulled into the flames. The fire flared, rising to touch the bathroom's ceiling, and then it died. The room went cool. And I shivered as I watched the woman float away on the smoke trailing out the open bathroom door.

I was expelled from school for two days for starting the fire. But I didn't care. Because after his talk with the school counselor, Dad postponed his next business trip to spend more time with me. All it took was one more fire to keep him home for my birthday. A birthday that was being ruined by stupid Grandpa and his stupid sheep. I pictured flames curling up into the sky when Dad said, "*Mintzazira ingeleses,* Aita. Speak English, Dad."

When I heard Dad speaking Basque, the vision in my head of me riding Legend City's roller coaster fifty times came to a screeching stop. Hearing Basque was never good. Dad only used it at the start of long arguments with Grandpa, and Oxea only spoke it when he was making fun of me.

"*Zendako* . . . why would you . . . *hori egin eni* . . . do this a me?" Grandpa said, his English breaking through in punches.

"Now, then, the sheep were worthless," Dad said.

"*Hori ezda hala,*" Grandpa said. "That no so."

"We couldn't afford to keep them, Aita."

That's what Dad said, anyway, but I knew the truth. Grandpa was getting old. Too old. The past year, he'd started to forget things. Like at the store he forgot that Oscar Mayer didn't make blood sausage, and at McDonald's he forgot that the girl with braces behind the counter had never heard of *txilindron*—lamb stew. And just last week Grandpa forgot that my mother was dead.

"Tell *zure ama*—your mother, she need come visit some time," Grandpa had said when he called on the phone to talk to Dad. I didn't say anything, I just rolled my eyes and handed the phone to my father.

Grandpa had turned eighty-one the month before, and Dad started talking about us moving back out to the farm to be with him. An idea I told Dad sucked big time, and I was sent to my room for expressing my opinion.

I looked from Grandpa to my dad now and said, "This isn't fair."

"*Ba*, yes, no is fair, sell *ene ardiak*," Grandpa said. "Sell my sheeps."

"Forget your stupid sheep," I said. "We were going to Legend City for my birthday—just me and Dad—and now you've ruined it."

"Sure, no, *zure* birthday?" Grandpa said. "Why no person remind I? *Orai*, I no have sheeps a give you."

That was when I quit listening and started thinking about all the ways I hated sheep—I hated the way they smelled like unwashed sweaters, and the way they bleated like babies with wet diapers, and I extra hated the way they looked at me with their big brown eyes that said, "You have to take care of me, I'm helpless." I hated and hated and hated. I needed to release my anger, and since I didn't have any matches, I decided to go pick a fight with Oxea. In the absence of fire, a good fight seemed the next best thing.

Oxea was Grandpa's little brother, only he was about a foot taller than Grandpa. And even though he was in his seventies, Oxea could place a walnut between his forearm and bicep and crack the shell by flexing his muscles.

"I like mountain," Oxea would say. "I made of stone."

And I'd agree and tell him I was sure his head was full of rocks.

Oxea loved sheep. He castrated them with his teeth and spit their testicles into a bloody bucket. Then he ate them as fried mountain oysters.

I told him that was sick.

He told me that they tasted like sausage dipped in sugar.

It was all part of our ongoing battle. One that started when I was seven and threw Oxea's beret onto the barn's roof. That was when Oxea told me about the Mamu, a giant, hairy creature.

"You mean Bigfoot?" I said.

"*Ez*, no," Oxea said. "The Mamu, he make you Bigfoot look like puppy."

"You're lying."

"You come see," Oxea said. "Mamu, he get hungry, he find you."

"Me?"

"Mamu, he like taste of bad little boys. They like *oilaskoa*—chicken to Mamu."

And even though I swore I didn't believe Oxea, for a month I had nightmares of long, hairy arms reaching around corners for me. Oxea told me other stories as well. Some I believed, but most—even at seven—I questioned. Like his telling me he could talk to sheep.

"Sheep don't speak Basque," I said.

"Not now," Oxea said. "Not after what snake he say to Eve. After then, God, he say, 'Not more animals they talk to men. *Orai*—now, only listen.'"

"No, God didn't," I said.

"*Ba*, you go, look in Bible, it say so."

And I had looked, and nowhere did I find anything about animals ever speaking Basque.

I went around the side of the house to where the barn was. I knew I'd find Oxea there, drinking red wine from his *zakua*—wineskin. He'd be all sad because of the loss of his precious sheep. I wished I'd had a Bible with me right then, because if I did, I'd pull it out and make Oxea show me where it said animals understood Basque. And when he couldn't, I'd tell him he was a mountain, all right, a mountain of lies. That would get Oxea so mad he'd tell me again how when I was born I was "*ttipia eta itsusia. Bildotza gaixua.*" Small and ugly. A runt lamb. And then we'd both yell insults at each other, he in Basque, me in English. Which was just what I wanted.

I was planning how I'd throw Oxea's *zakua* up on the barn's roof along with his beret when I passed the farmhouse with its crawl space beneath. I was sure Atarrabi and Mikelats would be sleeping in the damp dirt there, so I picked up the nearby hose. A blast of water would send the dogs bolting from their hiding place. The meaness of the idea made me feel a little better. I got on my knees with the hose in my hand and checked the crawl space. The dogs weren't there.

Maybe Dad had sold the dogs too. It would serve them right. Atarrabi and Mikelats were the two laziest dogs in the world, so lazy they didn't even bother to look different. Each had a long, usually mud-covered, gray coat, and each had one blue and one brown eye, and I couldn't tell the difference between the two dogs. They were supposed to be sheep dogs, only I'd never seen either one of them go near the sheep penned up next to the barn.

"*Ardiak nahi ditut gileat,*" I heard Grandpa yell at Dad. "I want sheeps back."

"They're gone," Dad said. "Now, then, there's nothing to do about it."

As Grandpa's voice rose even louder, I brushed the dirt from my hands and knees and headed toward the barn. I walked past the tractor that had been missing a tire since before I was born, and through the assortment of rusted equipment that seemed to be growing out of the ground. The arguing faded behind me as I neared the barn.

The barn door was open. I stepped inside. It was empty. Cracks of light fell through gaps in the barn's walls and onto the dirt floor. A broken bale of hay lay on a pallet. Clumps of wool were caught on the pallet's wood. The smell of sheep was in the air. But there were no sheep. No shuffling of hooves. No *baa*ing. It was quiet now.

"Oxea?"

My voice filled the barn.

"Atarrabi? Mikelats?"

Where were they hiding?

A gust of wind creaked open the door at the other end of the barn, and for some reason I thought of the Mamu. Was he lurking nearby? Waiting for me still? I told myself to stop being stupid. I was thirteen, too old to be scared by a kids' fairy tale. There was no Mamu. Oxea made it all up. Just the same, I decided to go back the way I came. As I was turning around, the wind gusted again. This time the barn's door swung wide open with a bang, and there, framed in the doorway, I saw the dogs. They were sitting in the middle of the pasture underneath the big oak.

"There you are, you lazy mutts," I said, but neither Atarrabi nor Mikelats seemed to hear me. Their attention was fixed on something in the oak. From where I stood, it looked like one of the tarps used to cover the hay had blown loose and gotten caught up in the tree's limbs. But then, as I stepped from the darkness of the barn into the light outside, I saw that it wasn't a tarp but a man. And I laughed at the sight of Oxea clinging to a limb of the oak.

"Oxea, let go," I yelled.

But he didn't.

Dry grass rustled beneath my shoes as I walked toward the oak. How was Oxea holding on so long? Atarrabi and Mikelats turned to gaze at me. One of the dogs whined.

"Oxe . . ." I started to say again, but stopped. There was something wrong about the way he was hanging on to the tree. For a moment I couldn't figure out what it was. I bit the corner of my lower lip. Moved closer. What was he doing up in the oak, anyway? Oxea must have lost it, just like Grandpa. All over some stupid sheep. But why climb a tree? Then I saw his hands. They were by his sides. Open. Empty. Holding nothing. My feet quit. I couldn't breathe. A second sun seemed to rise in my throat as I saw that the braided cotton rope Oxea used to hobble sheep was knotted around his neck.

Still, I didn't run for my dad, not yet. After all, this was Oxea, who told me animals understood Basque. That Mari, the queen of the genies, flew through the air in a ball of flames. That the *lamiak*, little people no bigger than my hand, snuck into my house each night and dreamed of being human.

I stepped closer.

Oxea hanging from the tree wasn't possible. Not Oxea. Oxea who could walk across the length of the pasture with a full-grown sheep under each arm. Oxea who could throw a bale of hay into the sheep pen with one hand. Oxea was made of stone. He was like the mountain, forever.

Oxea's eyes were open, and I waited for him to start laughing. To say, "Got you, *gaixua*." But his expression remained flat. The way he and Grandpa looked whenever I used the latest slang I picked up at school. The words put together in a jumble of English they couldn't untangle.

Flies buzzed through the air. They landed on Oxea's cheeks, which were as swollen and red as the blood sausage he loved to eat. A sour smell rose from the ground below his feet where wine puddled in the dirt. Oxea's beret lay there, next to his *zakua.* Wind blew through the oak so that the leaves seemed to whisper with a hundred voices as the limb Oxea hung from creaked like it was going to break. I watched Oxea swing back and forth, his body ticking off seconds to a birthday that was over before it started.

two | bida

That night I dreamed of the Mamu. I was at Grandpa's farm and it was dusk. Red light spilled out over the ground. Nothing moved. I called out for Atarrabi and Mikelats. But the dogs didn't come. They were hiding. And I knew what from.

I wasn't alone.

I walked up the driveway toward the farmhouse, past the place where Dad and Grandpa were arguing, on toward the barn. My heart quickened. There was still time. Things could be changed. If I hurried.

I started to run.

When I reached the barn, the inside smelled of Oxea—dusty wool and sour wine. I kept going. At the far end of the barn, I pushed open the door. The oak was waiting. The tree was as tall as the barn with a trunk as thick as my spread-out arms. Only the top of the tree didn't look solid, but like a puff of smoke that a strong wind could blow away.

There was nothing hanging from any of the oak's limbs. I let out the breath I didn't know I was holding. It was a dream. What had happened wasn't real. Oxea was alive. It was a dream. Then I heard something moving through the dead grass of the pasture. An arm slipped around the side of the oak. Clumps of what looked like wool stuck to skin as lumpy as the tree's bark. The arm reached toward me, and I saw that instead of claws on the large, flat paw, there were fingers, short and thick, like Grandpa's, Dad's, and my own.

I couldn't move. The top of a head appeared from behind the tree. I recognized Oxea's black curly hair and the red flush of his cheeks. Only his hair was longer now and all knotted together. It fell over his shoulders. And his cheeks were streaked with scars.

Then I saw his eyes. Oxea was and wasn't in those brown eyes. Oxea had become the Mamu. Or at least part of him had, and that part was wild and scared me.

The Mamu opened his mouth. His teeth were chipped, and only one of his canines was left. He threw back his head and let out a cry. It was the high, rising *irrintzina* that Oxea called to me with on the farm. The same cry Oxea told me sheepherders in the Basque Country used to call to each other across the Pyrenees Mountains. But the Mamu's *irrintzina* went unanswered. The Basque Country was an ocean away, and there were no sheepherders here, only me, and I stayed silent.

The Mamu cried again, and the power of his *irrintzina* shook the oak. I pressed my hands over my ears and fell to my knees. I didn't want to hear any more. Not because I was afraid but because of the pain in the Mamu's voice. It was like his heart was being crushed inside his chest. I shut my eyes as my body slid down into the ground where it became tangled within the tree's roots, and in the darkness there I heard the Mamu breathing.

I woke to find my father standing over me.

"What the hell?"

I sat straight up in bed. There was a spaghetti stain from last night's dinner on Dad's untucked shirt. Had he been standing there all night? His uncombed hair was pushed flat on his head.

"Good morning, Matt," Dad said.

"What are you doing?"

"Now, then, I have to fly to Denver in an hour," Dad said.

"Why?"

"Oxea wanted to be buried beside his wife."

"He was married?"

"Twenty-two years," Dad said. "It's a Catholic cemetery."

"So?"

"Because of the way Oxea . . . well . . . it happened, there are some legal issues that need to be straightened out."

"He was Grandpa's brother," I said. "Let him go."

Dad sighed. "My dad can't do it."

"How come?"

"Because he can't," Dad said.

His eyes were rimmed in red, and I didn't like to think he'd been crying. He pressed the palms of his hands against his forehead as if trying to keep something in there from spilling out, and at the sight of his hands, my dream came back to me.

"I'm going with you," I said.

"You have to stay here with Grandpa."

"I'm not going to the farm," I said, and my voice shook in a way I wished it hadn't. It wasn't that I didn't like Grandpa's farm. In fact, up until I was ten, whenever Dad went out of town for business, I stayed on the farm with Grandpa and Oxea. I always had a great time. But then one day at breakfast I told Dad I didn't want to stay there anymore.

"Why not?" Dad had asked as he glanced up from the spreadsheet on the table.

"It's boring," I said. "I can't hang out with my friends or go to the mall or ride my skateboard or anything."

Which was a lot less than half the truth. The rest being that I'd become aware of how different Grandpa was from other kids' grandparents. He made blood sausage and swore an inflated sheep's bladder was the best balloon. Other kids' grandparents' lives were about bridge games and trips to Mexico, but my grandpa's life was all about sheep. He was an embarrassing secret I was determined to keep. So Dad arranged for Mrs. Smith to stay with me whenever he was gone, and Grandpa never said a word about it. Whenever I did come to the farm, he acted like I'd always been there, just out of sight, around the corner but within calling distance.

"I'm not going to the farm," I said again. This time holding my voice steady.

"He's coming here," Dad said.

"Why can't Mrs. Smith stay with me?"

Dad shifted his weight from one foot to another, and I could see he was thinking about how to answer me.

"Matt, I'm worried about my father," Dad finally said. "You know how he gets confused sometimes, and . . . well. Now, then, can you look after him for me? Make sure he's all right. Do you understand? He just lost his brother."

"I don't want to stay behind," I said, but meant "I don't want him here."

That didn't mean I didn't love my grandpa. It was just that love wasn't something I thought about. At least not like that, anyway, and definitely not while the person was right there. How embarrassing would that be? To me, love was about feeling solid. And right then I wasn't solid. Oxea was gone, and he'd left a bunch of holes in me that needed filling. Which was why I didn't want Grandpa to come. He would bring Oxea with him into our house—Oxea's smell, his touch. Reminding me of how dangerous love was and of how because I loved Oxea there was less of me now.

"Now, then, you and Grandpa will both fly out Wednesday for the funeral," Dad said.

With a grunt, I threw my head back on my pillow and clenched my teeth.

Dad chuckled. "When you don't get your way, you stick out your chin like your mother did."

Without thinking, my hand went to my face. I pushed my chin back into place. Then, before I had a chance to turn away, Dad leaned down and kissed my cheek.

"I love you."

"Get out." I pulled the covers up over my head and kept them there until I heard the door shut.

An hour later as I walked to school, I reached into my back pocket and pulled out a photo of my mother. I'd stolen the picture from my dad's dresser after he left for the airport. I wasn't allowed in Dad's room when he wasn't home, and I certainly wasn't allowed to go through his dresser. So I did.

I again looked at the woman who was my mother. She was leaning out a pickup truck's window and waving her hand. In the picture, her hair flies like the pickup is racing forward. But it must be the wind, because the pickup's door is open and she is stepping out. Her face is turned to the side—something catching her green eyes. Whatever she sees is changing her expression. The camera clicked at a moment between happiness and—what? I didn't know.

What did she see? What took away her smile? I stared at the picture as I tried to fix the image of my mother in my head. But, like always, as soon as I stuck the photo back in my pocket, she began to fade, to again become just a woman I couldn't have picked out from a crowd.

Maybe it would have been different if I'd been older than two when Mom got struck by the car whose driver said he never even saw her. Or if Dad had talked more about Mom. Or if my mother's parents were alive and not buried in a cemetery somewhere in the Basque Country. In some ways, it was like she never existed.

I couldn't say the same thing about my grandpa. He existed all too much.

three | hiru

After lunch that day, Grandpa entered Ms. Helm's seventh-grade history class without even knocking.

Ms. Helm was in the middle of a lecture on the United Nations: "Established in 1945 at the end of the Second World War," Ms. Helm said, "the United Nations was designed to promote peace and understanding among the diverse cultures of our world."

Rich and I were at the back of class sniggering about how Mike Clausen looked mighty cute in the kilt he wore to school for Heritage Day when Rich elbowed me and said, "Where'd he escape from?"

I looked up to see Grandpa standing in the doorway.

I immediately hunched down low in my seat. I slipped the picture of my mother out of my pants pocket and into my desk. Then I closed my eyes. No way was he here. Please, God, I had to still be dreaming. Wake up. Just wake up. But when I opened my eyes, unlike the Mamu, Grandpa didn't disappear. I searched for a way to escape. But Grandpa stood in the only doorway, and all the room's windows were covered with screens. I was trapped.

"He looks like that guy in the World War II picture from our book," Rich said.

Grandpa wore his usual dusty black coat, which hung off his body like he was a boy who'd stolen it from his father's closet. Grandpa kept his eyes down as he shifted his weight from one foot to the other.

"I heard they were sending actors around for Heritage Day dressed up like they were from different countries," Linda Garcia said from the far side of Rich.

"Hey, Mike," Rich said, "why don't you go up and do a jig with the old guy?"

And the other kids in class laughed until Ms. Helm told them to be quiet.

"Can I help you?" Ms. Helm said to Grandpa.

Still not looking up, Grandpa held out a piece of white paper. When Mrs. Helm stepped out from behind her desk and walked over to take the paper, I heard Rich shift in his seat and knew that he and all the other boys in class were looking at her legs. Ms. Helm was right out of college and had great legs. Great legs being defined as not bony and short like those of the girls in our class. Ms. Helm's legs seemed to stretch on forever and you could see the outline of her calf muscles when she walked. Normally I took every chance I got to look at Ms. Helm's legs. But Grandpa in my classroom wasn't normal. So I kept my eyes on him—and let an opportunity to check out Ms. Helm's legs slip by—as I tried to will my grandpa to turn around and walk out the door before anyone found out we were related.

"I'm sorry," Ms. Helm said, "but we don't have a Mathieu Et . . . how do you say it?"

That was when Grandpa looked up. He hadn't shaved,

and I could see the gray stubble on his face. His cheeks were as red as burgundy wine, and his impossibly hooked nose looked like it could have doubled for one of the shepherd's crooks he kept in the barn.

"Etcheberri," Grandpa said. "It mean 'new house.'"

"Oh," Ms. Helm said. "How interesting. What language is that?"

"Euskara," Grandpa said. "Basque."

Everyone in class was murmuring. "Did he say bass?" "What kind of bass?" "I didn't know fish could talk."

Grandpa worked the edge of his beret through his fingers like a turning wheel, and I saw Ms. Helm's nose wrinkle slightly as she sniffed the air. She smelled the sheep. I slid down lower in my seat and prayed he would go away. But instead of leaving, Grandpa scanned the room. He must have recognized the top of my head, because he pointed and said, "Here Mathieu. My grandson."

All eyes in the class fixed on me.

"Matt?" Ms. Helm said. "Matt Echbar, please come up here."

I kept my head down and my own eyes on my classmates' loafers and Keds as I moved up the aisle to comments of "Hey, fish-boy, I got a worm for you" and "My kilt's looking pretty good now, huh?"

"I should have known your real name was Mathieu," Ms. Helm said as I stepped up to her desk.

I twisted my neck to the side and glared up at Grandpa as I bit my upper lip. But Grandpa was unaware of my pain. He smiled back at me.

"Sure, no, like mine," Grandpa said. "It family way. We . . . how you say . . . flip-flop oldest son name—Mathieu, Ferdinand, Mathieu, Ferdinand."

"Oh," Ms. Helm said, "how charming."

Grandpa held his beret to his chest and gave a little bow to Ms. Helm. And she laughed in a way that was more like a sigh than a laugh. Some of the girls in class started to clap. I squeezed my eyes shut and held my breath in hopes of passing out. But it was no use, I was forced to remain conscious while my seventh-grade reputation was ruined.

"I love your beret," Ms. Helm said.

"A Basque, he never without beret. Who know when it maybe rain."

"Hey, Matt, where's your beret?" Rich said from the back of the room.

"Quiet," Ms Helm said. "Matt, you never told me you were Basque."

"I must have forgot," I said.

"From your last name, I thought you were German," Ms. Helm said.

"Many Basques, when they come America change name, make easier on tongue," Grandpa said.

With my dad our name change was part of what he called his "career strategy." When he started working for John Deere our last name went from Etcheberri to Echbar. When I was old enough to realize that our last name was different than Grandpa's, I asked Dad about it. He told me he changed our name "because no one can say Etcheberri. Echbar is easier." And I accepted his explanation because Echbar was easier to say than Etcheberri. I never thought to wonder if there was another reason for Dad changing our name. Or to think about what part of the past disappeared with the letters he chose to leave out.

As far as being called Matt, well, everyone called me that—except for Grandpa, who insisted on calling me Mathieu, which I hated because it sounded like a name for a baptism or funeral and not one for the everyday world.

"Forgive me," Ms. Helm said, "I've heard of the Basque-land, but I'm not exactly sure where it is."

"Euskal Herria, we Basque call, it in Eden, in Pyrenees."

Some of my classmates hooted and called out, "Matt's from Eden."

"That's fascinating." Ms. Helm touched her lips with the tips of her fingers. "What else can you tell us about being Basque?"

"I tell how *neska*—girl like you make shepherd forget he got sheeps," Grandpa said. Ms. Helm giggled, and my stomach twisted like it was caught in barbed wire.

"Let's go," I said and took hold of Grandpa's coat sleeve.

"It nice meet you all," Grandpa said as I pulled him to the door. "Mathieu no tell how he got *polita*—pretty teacher. He only say some thing about legs. How that again, Mathieu?"

"Go," I said.

"*Izan untxa,*" Grandpa tipped his beret toward the class. "Be well."

And I heard Ms. Helm and the whole class say "*Izan untxa*" back, with a few "*Izan untxa,* Mathieu from Eden," thrown in as I pulled the classroom door closed.

"What are you doing here?" I faced off with Grandpa in the hallway outside my class.

"I get you," Grandpa said.

"After school—not in the middle of class," I said and heard laughter from inside the room that I was sure had to do with me being the bass-boy from Eden. "You totally humiliated me in front of everyone."

"How I do that?" Grandpa said, and I noticed the edge of a smile on his face.

"You know how."

"Sure, no," Grandpa said. "I only try make nice with *zure*—your friends."

He shrugged innocently.

"Yeah, great," was all I could think to say, since I didn't know if he was being straight with me. I could never tell with Grandpa—what he did and didn't understand, what he did and didn't mean to do. And if I kept asking him about it, he'd start with his not-knowing-English thing. Which I was pretty sure was bull but had no way of proving.

"We go back inside," Grandpa said. "I say sorry a teacher and *zu*—"

"No way." I blocked the classroom door. "Let's just go home."

I herded Grandpa down the hallway.

four | lau

Grandpa's '59 lime-green pickup was in the faculty parking lot. The rusted vehicle sat amid the teachers' shiny cars. Piled in the back were two bales of hay, rolls of wire, and the wooden posts of an old corral. I groaned. The Beverly Hill-billies. All I needed was for the kids in my class to see this. On top of the pickup's junk lay Atarrabi and Mikelats. Of course, both dogs were asleep.

"You can't park here," I told Grandpa.

"Sure, no, it parking place, *ba*—yes?"

"Faculty," I said. "Can't you read?"

"*Ba,*" Grandpa said, "*baina* only words I know."

As we got closer, I saw that Grandpa's pickup was right next to Principal Lench's Lincoln Continental. The silver car's paint glistened in the afternoon sun, as did the wet tires where one or both of the dogs had peed.

"Stupid dogs." I glared up at Atarrabi and Mikelats, who seemed to be grinning at me in their sleep.

I pulled open the pickup's passenger door, and the leg bone of a lamb fell out onto the asphalt. Besides being gross, the bone had to be for Atarrabi or Mikelats—not even my grandpa would gnaw on an old bone, at least I didn't think he would—and since I was mad at the dogs and Grandpa and his ugly pickup, I left the bone where it landed on the ground and got in.

As Grandpa climbed into the driver's seat, he said, "You got nice teacher. *Polita ba?*"

"School sucks."

"Like *bildotsa*—lambs on momma's teat?"

"You know what I mean."

Grandpa shook his head as he started the pickup.

"Sure, no, English so *gogora*—hard. Many words they sound same but no mean same."

"Go already."

I slumped down in my seat and pulled my shirt collar up to my chin. I checked the school's windows to see if anyone had watched me get into the pickup. Not that it mattered. I knew I was doomed to be the bass-boy from Eden for the rest of my school life.

The pickup's gears ground as Grandpa pulled out of the lot and onto the street. At the end of the block, a construction worker with a flag waved us on. They were working on the new Valley Bank building. Ms. Helm had told the class it would be the tallest building in Phoenix. Chunks of asphalt were piled up on the sidewalk, and the pickup vibrated with the noise of a jackhammer pounding the earth as Grandpa drove forward at a crawl. The red Buick behind us honked.

"Could you drive any slower?" I said.

"Sure, no, very hard drive this place," Grandpa said. "Glass all shiny, path very narrow, *eta* people they like sheeps got no shepherd."

"It's not like it's New York," I said. "It's just Phoenix. Geez, it's barely a city."

"It city enough," Grandpa said.

As we drove past the construction, I peered up at the building's steel frame rising toward the white sun. Right then, I wanted to be up there, on top, all alone, with nothing but blue sky around me—no school, no Rich, no Grandpa. Then I thought of Oxea. Was that what it was like for him now? Was Oxea floating somewhere in the clouds? Looking down and watching me? Wishing he could come back? Or was Oxea glad that he was gone?

When I glanced back over at Grandpa, it was like he knew what I was thinking. No muscles moved on his face, and his eyes didn't blink. I recognized that look. I'd seen it on Oxea's, Dad's, and even my own face. He was working out a problem. About his brother probably. Going over what happened. Trying to figure out a way to undo it. Or maybe not . . . maybe the hole Oxea left in Grandpa was too big to fill and Grandpa was thinking of following Oxea up into those clouds. I couldn't know, and Grandpa wouldn't tell me. We didn't do that in our family. We worked out our problems alone, without anyone knowing what was going on inside. But what if Oxea had told Grandpa what he was going to do? What would Grandpa have done? Could he have stopped his brother? Would Oxea still be here?

My head was hot with thinking.

I knew other families shared their feelings, sometimes even at the dinner table. I didn't want that. In fact, the thought of it made my stomach rise up into my chest, like it did when I jumped from the top of the monkey bars at school. It was bad enough in class where we were encouraged and sometimes even forced to express our feelings. And boy, did some of those kids express. Just that week, Missy McGregor told the class she needed everyone to say something nice to her because she was having a "low-self-esteem day." And Bobby Carrol announced that his bed-wetting had returned because he'd been picked last for baseball during recess.

Hearing my classmates say things like that made me feel like I'd vomited on myself. The one time Ms. Helm got me to "share" was still fresh in my mind. It was Personal History Day, and we were making memory books for our mothers, which I told Ms. Helm I couldn't do since I didn't have either a mother or any memories of her. Ms. Helm got all teary-eyed and stood in front of the class and said, "Everyone, I want you to give one of the memories you have of your mother to Matt so that he can fill his book."

I spent the rest of the day with kids coming up to me giving me memories of the time their mom put a cool towel on their head when they were sick and of their mom making chocolate chip cookies for them and reading to them at night and knowing magic words to make pain go away. And all the time I felt like I needed a shower.

But right then, riding with Grandpa in that pickup, I wanted him to do a little sharing with me. I remembered what Dad said, about how he was worried about Grandpa, and I couldn't stop thinking about Oxea hanging from the oak tree, swinging from side to side. I had to get out of myself, and for Grandpa to do the same, so I broke the family code and said, "You're not going to kill yourself, are you?"

Grandpa frowned.

"When you born, you *ttipia eta itsusia. Bildotsa gaixua.* Small and ugly. A runt lamb."

Grandpa said it like Oxea would—the words coming out one at a time. Oxea, who always spoke slow, each word a falling rock from his mouth, even when he was mad. Not like Grandpa at all, whose words bounced and tumbled against each other in their race to be heard. It was like Grandpa had become Oxea and Oxea him. The two of them living in the same body. And that didn't make me feel one bit better.

Then Grandpa started to sing a song whose melody I recognized from the radio. It was Donny Osmond's "Puppy Love." Only, like always, when Grandpa sang a song, he made up his own lyrics.

"*Gileat behatzen dut zer egina zen eta ene bihotzain mina,* and they call that puppy in love," Grandpa sang. "I see back how has gone before and my heart, it aches and they call that puppy in love."

I was certain he wasn't singing the right lyrics in Basque either and just making up any words he felt like saying. But I couldn't prove it because I didn't understand his "secret" language. Still, I did notice how the words he sang in Basque kept changing.

"*Ene bihotzain itxura,*" Grandpa sang. "The shape of my hea—"

"I hate that song," I said.

"Hate, that big word," Grandpa said. "Really two word—hat with the e."

"E is not a word."

"Sure, no, no is word in English."

He was goofing on me, so I didn't say anything back. I was glad at least that he was all Grandpa again—a Grandpa I decided to pretend wasn't in the truck with me. At least until we got home and I could escape into my room and really be alone. But if I was going to ignore Grandpa, I needed something to ignore him with, so I opened the pickup's glove box and went through the stuff inside. There was a broken army knife with nothing but a spoon left, a bunch of parking tickets that were yellow with age, and an old knotted rope. I went to work trying to untie the rope. But Grandpa wouldn't be ignored.

"You got hair like *neska.*"

I focused on pulling the largest knot loose.

"Sure, no, maybe you should wear dress," Grandpa said.

I couldn't get my fingers in between the cords of the knotted rope, so I tried to use my teeth. But that didn't work either; the knot remained tight.

"You make *polita neska,*" Grandpa said.

I threw the rope back into the glove box and closed it.

"Yeah, well, you smell like a sheep," I said.

"*Mil esker*—thank you," Grandpa said. "Sheeps smell good."

Now it was my turn to goof on him.

"Whatever, Grandpa," I said and watched a scowl start at the top of his forehead and work its way down to the tip of his chin.

"*Aitatxi niz,* Mathieu," Grandpa said. "I Aitatxi. I no Grandpa."

"In America, you're Grandpa."

He growled. This was far more fun than working on a knotted rope.

"This no right," he said. "We Eskualdunak—Basques."

"You're Basque," I said. "I'm American—McDonald's, Pepsi, Disneyland—and no *aitatxis.*"

"*Zure aita* should no allow this," Grandpa said.

"I don't have an *aita,*" I said. "I have a dad."

"You got Aita, you got Aitatxi."

"Nobody I know has an *aitatxi,*" I said. "Nobody on my baseball team and nobody at school."

"You special, then."

"Yeah, great," I said. "I tell my friends I have an *aitatxi*, they'll think I have some kind of disease."

"*Ene izena da Aitatxi,*" he said. "My name is Aitatxi."

"Whatever, Grandpa."

"Why you do this thing? You no call Amatxi, grandma. You no call Oxea, uncle."

"I was three when Amatxi died," I said. "I didn't know any better. And as for Oxea, well . . ."

I'd never really thought of Oxea as my uncle. That sounded too grown up. And Oxea was anything but grown up. He was the one that showed me how to burp my name and how to spit watermelon seeds from the hayloft onto the unsuspecting heads of Atarrabi and Mikelats. Oxea and I hung out together, fought together, and got into trouble together. Oxea was Oxea. The name fit him, just like his loving sheep and always being on the farm. I realized then that I'd never seen Oxea anywhere but on the farm. He'd never come to our house or gone into town with Grandpa. It was like the farm was the only place Oxea existed. Until he didn't exist anymore.

"This because *zure aita*, he forget Euskara." Grandpa's hands tightened on the steering wheel. "Ferdinand, he need remember he Eskualduna. And so need you, Mathieu."

"How can I remember something I never knew?" I said and was about to point out that Dad no longer even called himself Ferdinand but now went by Fred, when I had a better idea.

"I tell you what, Grandpa. I'll call you Aitatxi if you call me Matt."

"Matt, how kind of name that? Sound like bat. You no bat, Mathieu you name."

"It's Matt or you stay Grandpa."

I smiled. Ha, this time I was the smart one.

Grandpa pressed his lips together, and I thought he was going to spit on the windshield. Then he cocked his head as if knocking something loose inside, clicked his tongue, and slid his beret back so that a clump of his white hair stuck out. Then he whispered to himself, "*Mendia heltzen da urratz bat aldian.*" I had no idea what that meant, and right then Grandpa didn't seem to be in the mood to tell me. Instead he said, "You got you-self *tratua*—deal, Matt."

I couldn't believe it.

"I thought you said that was a bat?"

"Sure, no. You be bat-boy you want," he said. "And I Aitatxi. Now, say me."

My throat was dry.

"Go," he said. "We got good *tratua.*"

"Ai-ta-txi," I said and hated the way it made him smile. He'd done it again. Gotten the better of me, even with my own idea.

Aitatxi began to sing another Donny Osmond song, "The Twelfth of Never." Top 40 pop songs that were played to death on the radio were the only ones he sang. And I was sure he did that on purpose. He only used songs he knew I'd heard so that his changing the lyrics would bug me.

"*Ene sematxia ezda azeria bezain abila, eta ni baino abiloa izainen da* on the twelfth of never," Aitatxi sang. "My grandson is not as smart as a fox and will be smarter than me on the twelfth of never."

My jaw jutted out as I turned toward the passenger window. There had to be a way for me to outsmart the old man. I just needed to think. But my mind went white when I saw that we were headed the wrong way. I'd been so busy arguing with Aitatxi that I hadn't paid attention to where we were going. We were on the outskirts of Phoenix and nowhere near home.

"We're supposed to go to my house."

"*Ez,* I think no," Aitatxi said.

I pulled in a quick breath at the memory of the oak tree.

"I don't want to go to the farm."

Aitatxi reached over and put his hand on my leg.

"No worry, *gaixua.* We no going a farm."

"Then where are we going?"

"You like sheeps, Matt?" Aitatxi said and grinned.

five | borzt

I knew stealing the sheep back was a bad idea from the first, and I told Aitatxi so.

"Dad wouldn't like this," I said as he turned onto Highway 60.

"Aita, he no here," Aitatxi said.

"He's going to be mad."

"Then he no should sell sheeps."

Aitatxi had found out that Dad sold the sheep to the Outwest Dude Ranch in Wickenburg, thirty miles north of Phoenix. I didn't know what a bunch of make-believe cowboys would want with sheep. They couldn't ride them, or at least not very far. I'd tried that. Riding a sheep was like being on a barrel wrapped in a loose rug. Sooner rather than later you ended up facedown in the dirt. Maybe they were going to have a giant barbecue and eat the sheep. Oh, man, Aitatxi would be hopping like the earth was on fire if they did that.

Out my window, I watched as we passed the white wall that separated Sun City from the rest of Phoenix. A billboard said: RETIREMENT LIVING WITHOUT THE KIDS. Behind the wall, sun reflected off the red tile roofs of houses lined up in circles like the rings of a giant tree. The sudden ending of the wall made me blink as white brick was replaced by gray dirt. The wall curved away into the distance; scraped and leveled land lay outside it. Nothing grew there. A dust devil sprang up. It twisted into the air for a few seconds before falling back to the ground. After a while, the gray dirt turned to brown desert.

Adobe houses with sagging flat roofs appeared along the road. There were signs in front of the houses with the word ANTIQUES. The houses' yards were crowded with rusting buckets and pieces of machinery and broken furniture. In the window of one of the houses a lady wearing an Indian headdress watched us pass.

"Today night, we go into pens," Aitatxi said. "Atarrabi and Mikelats, they get sheeps out."

"That's your plan?" I said. "Those stupid dogs won't even stay awake long enough to get one sheep."

"You no get in way of *txakurrak*—dogs."

"Forget the dogs. We're going to end up in jail," I said. Then I repeated the words my father said to me every time I got into trouble at school: "You're too old to be doing this."

Aitatxi didn't say anything for a moment. And in that moment day turned to night. Shadows filled the pickup's cab. They crawled over Aitatxi's face. His eyes grew large and his face blurred into Oxea's. I pushed my back up against the passenger door.

"They're only sheep," I heard myself whisper.

Then Aitatxi smiled and became himself again. He looked over at me and said, "Sure, no, you right, we go home."

I relaxed.

"I think that would be best."

Only Aitatxi didn't slow down the pickup or start to turn around.

"*Ba,*" Aitatxi said. "You need go a school tomorrow day. See nice friends."

A buzzing filled my head at the thought of returning to Ms. Helm's class. I pictured the looks the other kids would give me with Rich saying stuff like "You never told me you came from Eden, Mathieu. So what's that Eve babe like?"

"You be sure say hello a *polita* teacher for Aitatxi," he said. "How you say about legs again?"

"How long will this sheep thing take?" I said.

"With Oxea, we climb mountain a *etxola*—sheep camp in three day."

Nobody at school knew about Oxea's dying. Not yet, anyway. But it would probably be in the newspaper tomorrow. None of my friends even knew I had an *oxea,* and now they—and everybody in Phoenix—were going to read all about him and how he . . . well, it was none of their business. Oxea belonged to me and my family, and I didn't feel like sharing him with anyone else. Only there was nothing I could do about it, except maybe not be there. Aitatxi's sheep drive would get me through the week. And, if I was lucky, while I was gone the Phoenix Suns would make the play-offs, or better yet the school would burn down and Rich and the other kids would forget all about me and Eden and Oxea.

"Only three days?" I said.

"You, me, we go *puxkat*—little bit slower," Aitatxi said. "Friday, eat lunch at *etxola.*"

"Where exactly is this *et-cho*—sheep camp?"

"*Ene etxola,* it north, in Bradshaw Mountains," Aitatxi said. "Oxea, he loves this mountains, he say like Pyrenees."

"But which mountain is the sheep camp on?"

"You come, you find," Aitatxi said.

"We're going to miss Oxea's funeral," I said.

"*Ez,* he no in Colorado. My brother, he up at *etxola.*"

I was pretty sure Aitatxi meant in spirit. That his brother wasn't actually waiting for us up at this *extola.* Still, I couldn't help imagining the Mamu-Oxea from my dream stepping out from behind an oak and crying out his *irrintzina.* I was thinking that maybe utter humiliation by the kids at school wouldn't be so bad when the spotlighted entrance of the Outwest Dude Ranch appeared up ahead. There would be no stopping Aitatxi now.

We pulled over to the side of the road.

"We wait it get darker," Aitatxi said. "Then we go get sheeps."

From under the seat, he pulled out a loaf of sourdough bread, a chunk of sheep's milk cheese, and his *zakua*—wineskin—which I knew was full of red wine.

"Damn," Aitatxi said. "I forget *lukainka*—sausage."

"Dad says adults shouldn't cuss in front of kids."

"On sheeps drive, they no *haurrak*—kids, only *gizonak*—men."

"Then give me a shot of wine from your *zakua.*"

"Sure, no, you only damn kid."

"How come you never cuss in Basque?" I said.

"They no such words in Euskara."

"Yeah, right."

"Euskara, it talked before peoples need such words," Aitatxi said. "Everything better back before then."

"Oh, yeah, living in caves was better."

"Sure, no, better than cities spreading over land like shit from sick lambs." Which only showed me he could use English just fine when he wanted to.

Aitatxi broke apart the cheese and bread, and in the darkness of the cab we ate it with our hands. He pulled a second *zakua* from under the seat and gave it to me. But when I squeezed the leather bag, a stream of water, not wine, shot into my mouth. When we were done, Aitatxi told me to feed Atarrabi and Mikelats.

"They got much work this night," he said. "We need *txakurrak* strong. I got *bida*—two lambs bones—under seat."

I reached under my seat as if I didn't know that one of the bones lay on the asphalt of the school parking lot.

"There's only one," I told Aitatxi.

I couldn't see his face clearly in the cab, but saw him shake his head as he muttered, "*Zahar ziak ez du deus hunik ikarri zen.*" He sighed. "Old age, it bring nothing good. They more bones in back. I plan for sheeps drive. *Baina* we use now."

Aitatxi told me where the bones were, and I got out of the pickup to get them. When I did, Atarrabi and Mikelats jumped off the pile of junk in the pickup's bed. With tongues hanging out, they watched as I pulled out the bones.

"Lazy dogs." I looked from one to the other, trying to figure out which was Atarrabi and which was Mikelats. But there were no differences between the two dogs; they were exactly alike. I threw them each a bone and heard their teeth gnawing them as I climbed back into the cab.

"Take," Aitatxi said as I closed the pickup door. Something blacker than the night was in his hand.

"What is it?" I said.

"He want you get."

The cheese and bread turned to stones in my stomach.

"Oxea?"

"It he beret," Aitatxi said.

All the air in the pickup's cab was suddenly gone, and Oxea was everywhere: scowling down at me after I threw his beret onto the barn's roof, laughing as I tried to blow a clear note on his *txistu*—flute, hanging there from the oak tree . . . forever . . . Oxea . . . gone. I couldn't speak. I couldn't breathe. I pushed open the pickup's door and fell out. My right knee hit the ground, and then I was up and running, back the way we came.

I ran down the middle of the road, the broken white lines passing under my feet, the lights of Phoenix glowing in the distance.

Home.

I wanted to go home. To be in my own bed and pull the covers over my head and go to sleep and wake up with Dad there and Aitatxi and his sheep on the farm and Oxea alive. Warm air stung my eyes, and I squinted as tears worked their way back along my face and into my ears. If I could just get home, then everything would be all right. Something grabbed at the cuff of my jeans. I looked down and saw Atarrabi and Mikelats running on either side of me.

"Go away." I kicked at one of the dogs. He dodged my foot as the other dog ran in front of me. I swerved to my left as he nipped my calf.

"Leave me alone," I yelled, but neither dog paid any attention. They just kept working their way around me, one in front, the other behind. To avoid the dogs' teeth, I head-faked and stutter-stepped like we learned in PE basketball. But I couldn't shake the dogs.

My side began to ache.

Finally, when the pain in my side cut right through the middle of my body, I stopped. Doubled over, I gulped for breath. Atarrabi and Mikelats walked past me without so much as a glance. Neither dog was even panting. When I raised my head to see where the demon dogs were going, I saw that I was back at the pickup. Aitatxi stood looking at me. Atarrabi and Mikelats went to lie at his feet. He didn't say anything, and I saw Oxea's beret was no longer in his hand. When I was able to stand up straight again, Aitatxi said to the dogs, "*Sartu*—get in."

Atarrabi and Mikelats jumped into the back of the pick-up, and Aitatxi went around to the driver's side. The pickup rumbled to a start.

I walked to the passenger door and climbed in.

six | sei

The cattle guard clanked beneath the tires of the pickup as we passed into the Outwest Dude Ranch. Aitatxi clicked off the headlights. In the moonlight I could make out a half dozen of the ranch's buildings up ahead. There were no lights on. Maybe the place was deserted. Maybe this wasn't where Aitatxi's sheep were after all. Maybe it had all been a big mistake.

Gravel popped beneath the pickup's tires. I wiped sweat off the back of my neck. We needed to just turn around and get the heck out of there. This whole thing was probably a trap, and I was sure we were going to get caught. Any minute John Wayne was going to ride up on horseback in a sequel to *The Cowboys*, only with sheep and not cattle surrounding him, and say, "What in hell do you fellas think you're doing?"

And I'd say, "It was the old man's idea. I'm innocent. Can I have your autograph?"

I leaned forward to look through the dead bugs on the windshield. My legs were shaking like electricity ran through them. At that moment, if someone had so much as touched me, I'd have launched myself straight through the windshield. I'd never been so excited in my life.

The main part of the ranch was a circle of bunkhouses. The shape of the bunkhouses reminded me of covered wagons, and I guessed that was the idea, the feel of the Old West. The rocking chairs on the bunkhouses' porches were all empty. A horse whinnied from a corral, but no one came in answer. In fact, there didn't seem to be a single dude on the dude ranch. Then I saw why. On the far side of the bunkhouses was the glow of a bonfire. "Home, Home on the Range" started up. The smell of steaks cooking was in the air, and my stomach growled for something more than bread and cheese.

Aitatxi drove the pickup into the middle of the circle of bunkhouses and parked.

"*Zure* pack in back." Aitatxi turned off the pickup. "For you, all thing in."

"You can't just leave your pickup here," I said.

"Sure, no."

"But they'll find it and know you took the sheep."

Aitatxi looked over at me, and even in the dark I could see his white teeth as he grinned.

"Gran—I mean, Aitatxi, you want them to know?"

But he didn't answer. He just got out of the pickup. The pack Aitatxi gave me was a lot smaller than the one he slipped on his back. Even so, when I pulled my pack on, it felt like a person was crammed inside. I'd have fallen over backward if Aitatxi hadn't steadied me with a hand on my shoulder.

"Keep forward, *gaixua,*" Aitatxi tightened my pack's leather straps.

"How far am I supposed to walk with this thing?"

"Soon pack, it like feather for you."

"A ton of feathers is still a ton," I said.

Aitatxi took his walking stick out of the pickup's bed. The stick was a foot longer than Aitatxi was tall. He gave a short whistle, and Atarrabi and Mikelats ran up. The dogs danced in front of Aitatxi like overcharged batteries. An hour earlier I wouldn't have believed either of them could be this wide awake. But now they seemed unable to contain the energy I figured they'd stored up from their endless sleeping.

"*Zazte ardien bila,*" Aitatxi said. "Go get sheeps."

The dogs took off. Aitatxi jogged after them, and I followed as best I could while trying not to fall over from the sliding weight of my pack. Something inside jabbed me in the back. Probably a wedge of cheese. I shifted the pack until whatever it was no longer pressed between my shoulder blades. Inside my pack, I smelled sourdough bread. Then I smelled something else—the sheep. It was like I stepped into a cloud of wet wool, dust, and piss. Up ahead, Aitatxi was already opening the gate to the pen where the sheep were. Atarrabi and Mikelats slipped inside and disappeared into the bleating wool.

"What do we do now?" I asked as the campfire group broke into "Happy Trails."

"We see," Aitatxi said. "Atarrabi and Mikelats, they do."

And he was right. Almost immediately the dogs began to drive the sheep out of the pen. The sheep filed past me, their *baa*ing rising to mix with the campfire group's singing. Dust filled my nose, and Aitatxi handed me a handkerchief. I saw how he had one tied over his nose and mouth. I did the same. One of the dogs ran past me and turned back the sheep headed toward the bonfire while the other dog finished emptying the pen. Then Aitatxi used his walking stick to close and latch the gate.

"*Joaiten gira,*" Aitatxi said. "We go," and he started walking away, out into the desert, leaving the sheep behind.

For a moment I stood where I was, confused. What about the sheep? After all this, was Aitatxi just going to leave them? But before I could say anything, Atarrabi and Mikelats began moving the sheep after Aitatxi.

While I ran to catch up with Aitatxi, I kept my eyes on Atarrabi and Mikelats. The dogs moved continuously around the outside of the sheep, keeping them together and driving them forward. Were these the same dogs I'd never seen do anything but sleep? The dogs that never even went near the sheep? Oxea was the one who loaded the sheep into the trailer-truck that he and Aitatxi drove up the mountain each year for the summer. All Atarrabi and Mikelats did was lie in the back of the pickup with their eyes closed. I never thought to wonder why Aitatxi and Oxea brought them along if all the dogs did was sleep. It seemed there was a whole other life of Atarrabi and Mikelats that I hadn't known about.

"Where are we going?" I asked when I caught up with Aitatxi.

"*Etxola*—sheep camp."

"I know that. But how are we going to get there? I mean, it's dark and all. How do you know if we're going the right way?"

Aitatxi used his walking stick to point at the sky.

"We follow *izarrak*—stars."

"And they'll lead us to the *etxola?*"

"They show way a *aritz ona,*" Aitatxi said.

"But we're already in Arizona."

"*Ez,* you need remember Euskara," Aitaxi said. "*Aritz ona*—good oak."

"They sound the same."

"They no is same."

"Fine, so now we're taking the sheep to a tree."

"*Ez,* we take sheeps a *etxola* that near *aritz ona,*" Aitatxi said.

"Oh, that explains everything," I said. "Is this the same *etxola* that you and Oxea drive the trailer-truck up to each year?"

"Sure, no."

"Sure, no—then where's the road?"

"We go on *isileko*—secret trail," Aitatxi said.

"There's a good idea. That way if we get lost, no one will be able to find us."

"Amatxi know."

"Amatxi?" She'd been dead for ten years.

"Sure, no, she all the time meet us by foot of mountain. She have *txilindron*—lamb stew, and *oilaskoa arno zurian*—chicken in white wine. That woman, she know how a cook."

"Aitatxi, how long ago was the last time you used this trail?"

"*Etzira orroitzen,*" Aitatxi said. "Don't you remember, Ferdinand?"

"I'm Matt."

Aitatxi shook his head and looked at me as if surprised to find me there.

"Matt? How kind of name that? Like bat."

"Yeah, bat-boy, that's me," I said.

"Sure, no, Mathieu, you never go on sheeps drive."

"When was the last time you took the sheep this way, Aitatxi?"

"My brother, he lift up ram in each arm," Aitatxi said. "Oxea, he true *artzaina*—shepherd. He be sad he no here. *Baina,* Oxea, he wait for us up at *etxola.*"

Aitatxi was just confused. Like when we went to Kmart

and he spoke to the checkout guy in Basque, and the guy said, "What the heck you saying?" And Aitatxi blinked like he was waking up, then laughed, and said, "Sure, no, we in America now."

I just needed to get him to focus.

"Was I born the last time you used this trail, Aitatxi?"

"*Zer? Ez, zure aita,* he no even marry pretty little *neska.* We go before then."

"How long before then?"

"Year crazy Russians put dog up in sky. Poor *txakurra.*"

"Oh, my God," I said and remembered how the whole class at first laughed when Ms. Helm told us about the Soviet Union putting a dog named Laika aboard *Sputnik 2.* But the laughter stopped when Ms. Helm went on to tell us the satellite was not made to support life and that Laika died. "Where's the Humane Society when you need them?" Rich said.

That happened in 1957. Sixteen years ago.

seven | zazpi

The day Dad turned forty, we walked on the moon with Neil Armstrong. I was in my bedroom working on a report for Ms. Helm's class about the Cuban missile crisis. My report was already three days late, and Ms. Helm told me that if I didn't turn it in first thing in the morning, I'd get detention. Detention seemed unavoidable, since I hadn't written a word about Cuba or Castro or Kennedy or any missiles and didn't plan to. The whole thing was boring and had nothing to do with me. Why couldn't I write about something that was going on now? Like the Miami Dolphins' perfect season? Or Evel Knievel's motorcycle jumping over fifty-two cars?

I was flipping through my history book thinking what a waste of time history was when I came to the picture of the first moon walk. The image filled the page. I moved my book under the desk light to get a better look as I ran my fingers over the picture. The coolness of the moon seemed to come through the paper. Neil Armstrong stood in his space suit saluting. The gray mountains behind him looked like the Estrellas south of Phoenix at dusk. From the city, like the moon's mountains, the Estrellas appeared lifeless. But I knew they weren't. I'd seen pictures of the mountains' slopes in *Arizona Highways.* They were covered with cactus and trees and animals—some as big as deer. It was just that because of the distance I couldn't see those things from my house.

In the book's picture, an American flag seemed to be blowing in a wind I had learned in science class didn't exist. And there was part of what looked like a cheap kid's model of a spaceship off to the side. The ground at the astronaut's feet was marked with footprints, which I thought made it funny that the caption read, "One small step for man, one giant leap for mankind." Obviously there'd been a lot more than one step taken on the moon by the time the picture was snapped.

"Do you remember wanting to go live on the moon?" Dad said from behind me, and I nearly fell out of my chair at the sound of his voice.

"Geez," I said. "Don't do that."

"Sorry," Dad said and ran a hand through my hair.

"I never wanted to live on the moon." I started to shut the book, but Dad slipped his hand between the pages.

"You wanted to be an astronaut." He leaned over my shoulder to look at the picture of the moon walk, and I smelled the burned potatoes from dinner and dust and sweat from work on his shirt.

"I don't remember," I said.

"I do," Dad said. "But didn't every kid in America dream of being an astronaut that day?"

I looked up into my dad's face. He was smiling, and I saw how his front teeth were a little pushed together and not quite even. His eyes and skin were the brown of my oiled baseball glove, and his eyebrows, like his dad's, were thick and wild.

"After the telecast," Dad said, "Oxea helped you build a spaceship out of wooden pallets in the barn. Me and Aitatxi watched as Oxea did the countdown for your reentry into Earth's atmosphere." Dad held up ten fingers and began curling them down one at a time as he counted back, "*Hamar, bederatzi, zortxi, zazpi, sei, borzt, lau, hiru, bida, bagno—joan*—go! And you jumped from the loft into a pile of hay."

"Did I get hurt?"

"You were grinning from ear to ear when you popped up through the hay. And you kept saying, 'Did you see that, Dad? Did you see that? I'm as-trow-nut. I'm going to live on the moon.'"

"I did not," I said.

"Now, then, you think I'd kid about something like my son being an as-trow-nut?" Dad laughed as he fell back onto my bed. "Boy, I would have liked to have gone to the moon with you and Neil. Maybe I should've been an astronaut."

Dad an astronaut? The thought that my father could be something other than what he was had never crossed my mind before.

He lay there on my bed twisting a piece of paper between his fingers and looking out my bedroom window up at the full moon. He looked young then. Younger than forty. Like a kid. And happy. I wanted him to stay that way; not forever—with Dad and me, forever didn't seem possible. But right now did. So I lay down beside him, because it was his birthday and he was forty and a tractor salesman and not an astronaut.

"Houston, this is *Apollo 11* coming up on the moon," I said.

"Now, then, that's a copy." Dad put his arm around my shoulder. "I've got the lunar object in sight. What say we bring her in for a landing?"

"Ten-four," I said.

Dad and I flew to the moon that night, and for a few moments, time stopped and we floated together in weightless space.

I was thinking about Dad and Neil Armstrong as I followed Aitatxi further into the desert. Unlike Neil, I didn't have a radio to call home with. There was no way to let Dad know what was going on. He wouldn't even know Aitatxi and I were gone. He'd call the house and get no answer and probably think we were out for dinner. He might call Mrs. Smith to check on us, but that wouldn't be until morning. Mrs. Smith would knock and knock on the door and finally let herself in with the key Dad had given her. When she found no sign that we'd been there, she would call Dad and tell him something was wrong.

And by then something really might be wrong.

Dust from the moving sheep floated in the air around me. I retied the handkerchief over my nose and mouth and wished Dad had become an astronaut. Because if he had, then we'd live in Florida, and I was pretty sure there were no sheep on the beaches there.

Ahead of me, Aitatxi kept his eyes on the sky. I looked up at the same stars uneasily. They seemed brighter here than in the city. And closer. In their glow, the desert was as lit up as a parking lot. And while maybe that was nice to be able to see where we were going, it only left me longing for the streetlights of the city. Aitatxi, on the other hand, seemed to be fascinated by the closeness of the stars. As he walked, he moved the tip of his stick from one star to the next, as if he were connecting them.

A coyote's howl, sounding like a woman screaming, rose to sharpen the points of the stars.

"You hear that?" I said.

"No worry, *gaixua,*" Aitatxi said, "Atarrabi and Mikelats no let coyote get our sheeps."

"Forget the sheeps," I said. "What about me?"

"Coyote no like how little boy taste."

"Very funny," I said. "You sure you know where you're going?"

"*Ez, baina izarrak* know, *gaixua.*"

"The name's Matt, Grandpa," I said.

"Sure, no," Aitatxi said and muttered something about a bat. Then added, "You know name of *izarrak?*"

"Well"—I scanned the sky—"I know the brightest one is called the North Star."

"*Ez.*" Aitatxi pointed to a star on the horizon flickering brighter than the other. "That *izarra,* it Amatxi."

"Huh?"

Aitatxi pointed to another star directly above me.

"And that *izarra,* it *zure ama*—your mother."

I looked over at Aitatxi, expecting to find him grinning at me, sure he was goofing on me again. Only Aitatxi wasn't grinning. Instead, he was staring up at the sky with his lips pressed together, concentrating.

"And *zu* see," Aitatxi said, "that *izarra,* it Oxea, *ene anaia*—my brother."

"People don't become stars when they die, Aitatxi," I said. "They go to heaven."

"Being *izarra* it like heaven."

"You're losing it, Grandpa," I said, and my use of "Grandpa" made Aitatxi look away from the stars and glare at me.

Good. As long as Aitatxi was mad at me, he wouldn't talk to me. Which was just how I wanted it. I wouldn't have minded hearing how people became stars back home in the city. But out here in the desert, the thought of stars being dead people staring at me only filled my head with images of bony hands reaching down from the sky. I didn't need that. I was already freaked enough about being in the desert. Even though I'd lived my whole life in Phoenix, which was in the middle of a desert, that didn't mean I ever went into it. In fact, at school we were warned NOT to go into the desert. Especially alone. Things happened there. Bad things. Every summer it seemed the police would find a man, or a couple, sometimes even a whole family, whose car broke down on a dirt road that led nowhere and who'd tried to walk out, gotten lost, run out of water, and died of thirst.

Thinking of people dying of thirst made me thirsty. I should've looked for a water faucet back at the dude ranch. Who knew the next time I'd get a chance for a good drink? The inside of my throat felt like it was covered with dust. Had Aitatxi remembered to bring enough water? I was about to ask him when something swooped toward my face and I heard a high, squeaky cry.

"Bats!" I yelled.

Dozens of black shapes darted between the stars. I dropped to the ground with my arms covering my head.

Aitatxi laughed.

"They no bats, *gaixua*. They nighthawks. They good. Eat mosquitoes."

With my arms still over my head, I watched as the birds glided above the white backs of the sheep. I lowered my arms. If sheep weren't scared of these things, then I wasn't going to be. Of course, maybe sheep were too stupid to be scared.

"How much water did you bring?" I said as I got to my feet and beat the dust off my pants.

"I bring you *zakua* full."

"I'm thirsty."

"You no thirsty," Aitatxi said.

"I know when I'm thirsty."

"You only think you thirsty," Aitatxi said. "Wait *puxkat*—little bit. When *eguzkia*—sun—come up tomorrow day, hot like fire in hell, *eta* you mouth it feel like full of wool, then you thirsty. I give you *zakua* then."

"And what if I die of thirst before then?"

"I leave you for bats eat, no problem," Aitatxi said and led me further into the desert.

eight | zortzi

As we walked, I asked Aitatxi questions, like "You think maybe we should go back and tell them it was all a joke?" and "Do you know the prison time for stealing sheep?" and "How about if we get caught, I say I was kidnapped and you say aliens forced you to do it?" and "Don't sheep need to sleep?" But Aitatxi only answered me in Basque. The same language he spoke to Atarrabi and Mikelats. Unlike me though, the dogs seemed to understand every word as they moved the sheep forward in a tight bunch.

Finally, when every step was like sharp stones on my feet, I said, "When are we going to stop?"

And Aitatxi answered me in English, "Here is good."

He whistled to Atarrabi and Mikelats, then climbed down into a dry wash that a moment before I hadn't even seen. I followed Aitatxi down the slope. At the bottom, my feet sank into sand. Aitatxi handed me the end of a piece of rope. He pointed to a dead tree that was wedged up against the side of the wash.

"Tie a tree, low and hard," Aitatxi said.

"What for?"

"We no want sheeps run away at the night," Aitatxi said as the dogs moved the sheep down into the wash.

Right then, I didn't care if the sheep ran away or not. They were just sheep. Stupid sheep. In fact, if they were gone, then we could go home because what sense was there in Aitatxi going on his sheeps drive without sheeps? But then, what sense was there in pulling your grandson out of school, stealing thirty-two sheep, and taking all of them into the middle of the desert? Aitatxi sense, I guessed.

Beyond the dead tree, the wash turned so that its side swung wide to form a pocket. Atarrabi and Mikelats drove the sheep into the pocket and kept them there while I tied my end of the rope to the tree. But I tied the rope "low and soft," not "low and hard" like Aitatxi said. I planned to be extra sorry when the sheep were all gone in the morning.

Aitatxi tied his end of the rope onto a rock on the far wall. Then he pulled out a second rope and came back over to me to check my knot.

"You no tie so good, *gaixua*," he said as he tightened my knot.

"I flunked knot tying in Boy Scouts."

"Sure, no, you lucky I here a help you."

"Yeah," I said. "Super lucky."

Aitatxi tied the second rope to the tree a couple feet above the first. Atarrabi and Mikelats jumped through the two parallel ropes. Then Aitatxi took a third rope and wound it back and forth to fill the space in between. When he was done with his rope fence, there was no way the sheep were getting loose.

"Good camp," Aitatxi said. "*Ez?*"

"What if there's a flash flood?"

"Sure, now, then we be like Noah and build us ark."

Aitatxi pulled from his pack two lamb bones for Atarrabi and Mikelats.

"I make *sua*—fire," Aitatxi said. "You get ready for *bu-ba*—sleep."

"*Bu-ba?*" I said. "I haven't heard that since . . ."

"Since when?" Aitatxi said.

"Since never." I shook the word out of my head, along with the memory of someone leaning over me, a voice whispering, a cool hand on my forehead, a soft blanket tucked under my chin. "Forget it."

I reached into my pack to get out my bedroll and found Oxea's beret there. Aitatxi must have stuck the beret into my pack without me seeing. Couldn't he just leave me alone? Still, I didn't say anything. I just ran the soft fabric of the beret between my fingers. *Bu-ba.* I left the beret in my pack and pulled out my bedroll.

The fire was crackling, and in its glow I eyed the dogs' lamb bones, jealous of any scrap of meat that was on them. Aitatxi and I had a dinner of sheep's milk cheese and sourdough bread.

As we ate, Aitatxi asked if I wanted to hear the story of Mari. I already knew a little about Mari from Oxea. He told me Mari was the mother of the Mamu and that she had a hairy back and bowlegs. When I asked Oxea if maybe he wasn't confused and talking about one of his old girlfriends, he threw his *zakua* at my head.

"You've never told me a story before," I said to Aitatxi.

"I always tell story."

"No, you don't," I said. "Only Ox . . ."

"Sure, no," Aitatxi said, "*baina* before now, *gaixua*, Oxea, he tell you story. *Orai* I tell."

"Fine, just as long as there are no dead people in it."

"Sure, no, every people, they stay living."

"Okay, but if I don't like it, you have to stop."

"Sure, no," Aitatxi said.

I only agreed to listen to Aitatxi's story because anything was better than thinking about how much trouble we were going to be in for stealing the sheep and how I hadn't exactly "looked after" Aitatxi the way Dad asked me to and how we were probably lost in the desert and how we most likely didn't have enough water and . . .

"Start talking," I said.

"Mari, she queen of all genies," Aitatxi said. "She fly through air in flames of fire, and she rule over all rains."

A coyote howled. The sheep bleated. In the darkness I could no longer see them, but I sure could smell them. Or maybe it wasn't the sheep I smelled. I lifted the front of my shirt and sniffed. The stink of wool filled my nose. I sneezed. I'd become a stinking sheep.

"Mari, she live in all caves in world and fly from cave *eta* cave in gush of wind."

"I thought you said she flew in the flames of a fire?"

"No talk *ene* story," Aitatxi said.

I sighed. There was no getting Aitatxi to make sense of anything. I glanced down at Atarrabi and Mikelats. Each of the dogs had his head resting on one of my shoes like it was a pillow. Great watchdogs. I kicked my feet, and Atarrabi and Mikelats momentarily woke up. But it didn't last. They settled their heads onto the dirt and went right back to sleep.

"Mari, she one time regular girl," Aitatxi continued. "*Baina* she very naughty, and so her *ama*, she let Mari be taken by dark one."

"Who's the dark one?"

"You know, down below."

"The devil?"

Aitatxi nodded, "Deabrua."

"I don't think I like—"

"*Isilik*—be quiet," Aitatxi said. "I getting a good part. Mari, she dressed in pure white and has no sin. She hold child of God in hands. An—"

"That's the Virgin Mary, Aitatxi."

"Sure, no. Mari, she one time Blessed Virgin. One time Amatxi. And one time, Mari, she *zure ama.*"

At the mention of my mother, my face grew hot.

"*Zure ama,*" Aitatxi said. "She very *polita.*"

Mom. My eyes got all moisty. Instead of wiping my eyes with my hand, I blinked fast and stared into the fire. But the flames stayed empty—the woman's face wasn't there.

"Once time there handsome shepherd, he fall in love with Mari. But she no love him. Mari, she wind that no stop blowing. *Baina* shepherd, he no care. He in love. So he sing for Mari every night when she go by. Shepherd, he sing about *izarrak* and *illargia*—stars and moon. About *ura*—water that go out a sea. And *eguzkia*—sun, that burn all day. Mari, she act like she no listen. *Baina puxkat* by *puxkat,* her *bihotza*—heart, it change. And Mari, she know love. And winter it become like spring, and Mari, she and shepherd, they marry. And they so happy, they want more happiness. *Halala*—that way always is. So Mari, she and shepherd, they take little bit *izarrak* and little bit *illargia* and little bit *eguzkia* and make them boy. And they bring alive with *ura.* And Mari, she and shepherd, they name boy."

"What did they name him?"

"Mathieu."

The night was silent. Even the sheep had stopped their *baa*ing. I looked across the flames of the campfire and saw Aitatxi watching me. It felt like a rock was stuck in my throat, and I had to swallow hard to get it loose.

"You want Mari come," Aitatxi said, "you got call her three time. And when Mari, she come, you got a give her gift. Gift, it need be thing . . . how you say . . . worth much for you. Say maybe like good ram."

"You give her a sheep?"

"Sure, no."

I laughed, and Aitatxi grinned.

"Ram, it very good thing. No ram, you no got *bildotxak*—lambs."

"What if you don't happen to have a sheep with you?"

"Then give thing from *bihotza,*" Aitatxi said. "The heart, *gaixua.*"

"How do you say that again?"

"*Bihotza.*"

"*Bee-hot-sa.*"

"*Bee-ho—ts—a,*" Aitatxi said.

"I can't say that."

"Sure, no, you try, *berriz*—again."

"No," I said. "I'm too tired."

"*Ba,* time for *bu-ba.*"

I rolled my bedroll out on the sand and climbed in.

"So do you or the stars or the moon or the sun know where we are going tomorrow?"

"We going a *isileko* trail," Aitatxi said.

"And you're sure you know where this secret trail is?"

"Sure, I know," Aitatxi said.

"Where?"

"*Baina* I tell you, then no is secret. *Gauhon*—good night, *gaixua.*"

And with that, Aitatxi stretched out on top of his bedroll and covered his face with his beret.

After a couple of minutes, I heard him snoring. Only then did I reach into my pack and take out Oxea's beret. I placed it over my face like Aitatxi, and breathed in what smelled like a sweater dipped in sour milk. I smiled and closed my eyes.

"*Bee-ho—ts—a,*" I said, the beret's fabric brushing over my lips.

nine | bederatzi

I woke with sand in my mouth and one of the dogs licking my face. I pushed him away as I sat up to see the other dog lying on my bedroll. I must have rolled off in my sleep—or more likely been pushed off by Atarrabi and Mikelats. One of them had Oxea's beret hanging from his mouth.

"Give me that!" I grabbed the beret from either Atarrabi or Mikelats—I still couldn't tell the difference between the two of them—and put it on my head. "Stupid dogs."

I tried to spit, but the wool Aitatxi said would fill my mouth had arrived. I wiped my tongue off with my shirt. Three more days of this was going to suck big time. I shook sand out of my hair and brushed it off my cheek as I shivered. All night I'd frozen, and I woke up about a million times to the howls of coyotes. Each time the howls sounded closer, and I was sure the coyotes were moving in to rip out my throat. I was tired and hungry and cold, and it was all because of Aitatxi.

Aitatxi, who I realized as I looked around was gone. Great.

The sheep started *baa*ing behind me, and I heard the soft "*hoo-hoo*" of what sounded like an owl. Only I'd never heard an owl in the day before; in fact, I'd never heard one anywhere but on TV's *Wild Kingdom*. When I got to my feet to stretch, three doves flew up from the sand in front of me. The birds rose in a cloud of dust that hung in the air. They *hoo-hoo*ed as they flew into the sky, and I wondered at doves that sounded like owls.

My back and shoulders burned from carrying the pack. The sun hadn't gotten above the top of the wash, and I was already thirstier than I'd ever been. And where was Aitatxi? He'd gone off and left me alone with the sheep, who all seemed to be looking at me as if wondering, "Who the heck are you? Where's the old guy in charge? And what's for breakfast?"

I was thinking the same thing as I looked down the wash. In the morning light, everything was the color of the ashes from last night's campfire. The uprooted trunks of trees were scattered along the wash, whose sand was covered in ripples of wavy lines like flowing water.

Water. Just thinking about it made me thirstier. I spotted the *zakua* lying beside Aitatxi's bedroll. Since he wasn't around, now was the time to get a good drink. I took a step on stiff legs toward the *zakua*. I hit my thighs with my fists to get some feeling back into them and tried to brush off my pants, but it was no use. My legs stayed wooden, and the dirt on my pants was permanent.

I picked up the *zakua*, lifted it to my mouth, and squeezed the leather bag. Only instead of water, warm red wine shot into my mouth. I spit it out.

"I got *zakua* with *ura*," Aitatxi said, and I looked up to see him on the rim of the wash. He held the *zakua* with the water above his head.

I was about to say, "I hope you didn't drink it all," when the sun moved up behind Aitatxi to surround him with light, and, for a moment, it was like he was standing in the middle of the sun. His clothes were covered in flames, and the *zakua* he held in his raised hand glowed like a sword of fire. And as I stood there staring up at this changed Aitatxi, I thought of my father. Something from a long time ago. I was just a baby. Mom was still alive. She was near. I felt her warmth in the air. But I was watching Dad, looking up at him. His head seemed to rise into the clouds. Light surrounded his face. He was smiling, his hands reaching down for me. I grabbed for those hands—hands that could crush mountains, and take me up, up, up into a sky of fresh-cut alfalfa and the feel of razor stubble on my skin. I was happy, and I thought, "Mine. This is mine." But then it all changed. Mom died. Dad shrank. He no longer rose into the clouds, and until right then I'd forgotten that he ever did. The sun moved higher, past Aitatxi, and he once again became a little old man holding up a *zakua.*

"Nothing like firm pee a say good morning," Aitatxi said as he started down the side of the wash toward me.

"Sick."

"You see," Aitatxi said. "Forty, fifty year, you happy you get one."

Aitatxi handed me the *zakua* with water in it. I held it at arm's length and squeezed. Clear water shot out onto the sand.

Aitatxi looked at me. "Why you waste *ura?*"

"Just checking." I raised the tip of the *zakua* to my lips and filled my mouth with water. I would have kept on drinking until my stomach swelled, but Aitatxi didn't let me.

"No so fast." Aitatxi took the *zakua* away from me. "We

got go day more find trail. After then, it half day a where Oxea find *iturritza* . . . how you say . . . no-can-see water that come up from ground."

"You mean a spring?"

"*Ba,* no thing *baina* desert before *iturritza*—no-can-see *ura.*"

"What about the sheep?"

"Sheeps, they fine," Aitatxi said. "Sheeps, they no got a drink so much water like little boys. *Baina* you no worry, we no got *ura,* they plenty wine."

"No, thanks," I said.

"*Untxa*—good, more for me," Aitatxi said. "Now we go."

We rolled up our bedrolls and repacked our packs.

"Does Dad know about this secret trail we're going on?"

"Sure, no," Aitatxi said as we moved over to the rope fence holding in the sheep. I at first took his answer for "yes," but then realized it was as much "no" as "yes." I needed a solid answer from Aitatxi. A real yes or no.

"Aitatxi, wh—"

"Untie low rope first," Aitatxi said. "Understand, *gaixua?* No unti—"

"I know how to untie a rope," I said.

"Sure, no."

"What do you mean by that? Yes I do or no I don't?" I said and yanked loose the top rope. The fence collapsed all at once and the sheep poured out like water and raced down the wash.

"You no listen how I say?" Aitatxi said. "Low rope first."

"Sure, no," I yelled as I ran with the dogs after the sheep.

Fifteen minutes later, when Atarrabi and Mikelats finally got the sheep back together, instead of apologizing for what I'd done, I said, "When we get to the *etxola,* I hope I never see this bunch of sheep again."

"Bunch of sheeps? You no know English, I teach. It call flock."

"Flock is for birds."

"You English, it strange language," Aitatxi said. "No as beautiful as Euskara."

"Oh, yeah, you and Oxea with your *ba* this, *ba* that—*ba, ba, ba*. You guys sound like a flock of sheep."

"*Mil esker,*" Aitatxi smiled.

"You don't even know when you're being insulted," I said.

"Sure, no," Aitatxi said. "You no know when insulting."

"Forget it."

And with that we were on our way.

As we walked, whenever the flock started to spread out, Aitatxi called to the dogs in Basque.

"Atarrabi *zaza harat*—go there."

"Mikelats *zaza giletik*—go from back."

Finally I asked Aitatxi, "How can you tell them apart?"

"Atarrabi and Mikelats?"

"They look exactly alike."

"*Ez, txakurrak,* they different like *egun eta gau*—day and night," Aitatxi said and pointed to the dog off to my right. "See, Atarrabi, he keep tail low so you no can know how he feeling. *Baina* Mikelats"—Aitatxi pointed to the other dog at the front of the flock—"he tail most always going. If no, he sad. Very easy a know how Mikelats, he feel." As Aitatxi watched Mikelats, he shook his head disappointedly. "I think Mikelats, he learn that from some American dog."

"So you tell the difference between the two dogs by their tails?"

"That only one thing," Aitatxi said. "Atarrabi *eta* Mikelats, they very . . . how you say—no-like-same *txakurrak.*"

"Opposite dogs?" I said.

"*Ba,* Atarrabi, he dark inside like old man who live in cave. Mikelats, he light inside that no ever go out. You see?"

"Sure, no," I said. But then I looked at the dogs again, and I don't know if it was because of what Aitatxi said or not, but Mikelats did seem to jump along almost like he was skipping. And now that I looked closer, Atarrabi's whole body seemed to scowl.

"Together, two good *txakurrak,*" Aitatxi said. "*Baina* one with no other, I no think they so good."

"Why not?"

"*Egun eta gau,*" Aitatxi said. "Day no good no night."

I guessed he was right. I mean, if it was day all the time then when would I sleep? And if it was night all the time, then all I'd do was sleep. I knew there was probably more to what Aitatxi was saying than that, but right then I didn't ask him to go on about it. I had another question on my mind.

"Do dogs really understand Basque?"

"Sure, no. All animals, they know Euskara."

"Then why don't you tell the coyotes to stay away?"

"Coyotes, they like little boys, they no always listen," Aitatxi said, and I pretended not to see the wink he gave me. "You want try?"

I thought about it for a minute. It would be fun to get Atarrabi and Mikelats, who never did what I told them, to listen to me.

"Okay."

"Then you say, 'Mikelats *haugi hunat*—come here, boy.'"

"Mikelats how-gee," I said. And the dog's ears stood up.

"*Berriz*—again."

"Mikelats how-gee."

This time the dog sprinted over to me like I was pulling him on a chain.

I smiled. "Cool."

"*Zaza zuzen,*" Aitatxi said. "Go straight." And Mikelats ran to the front of the flock.

"How do you say, 'Stand on your head and pee'?"

"No is game, *gaixua,*" Aitatxi said. "We working here."

"I know," I said, even though I thought that command—though maybe not useful in keeping the sheep together—was something I'd love to know. "Then how do you tell them to stop?"

"*Geldi,*" Aitatxi said.

"Gel-dee? I've heard that word before."

"*Untxa.*" Aitatxi tilted back his beret. "Maybe you know from time *zure ama* speak Euskara when you baby."

"You heard my mom speak Basque?"

"Beautiful Zuberuan," Aitatxi said. "It like music come from her lips."

"Not like your singing, I hope."

Aitaxi decided not to listen to my comment.

"Did Mom talk to you in Basque?"

"Sure, no, I *eta* Oxea *eta* Amatxi *eta zure aita.*"

"Dad doesn't speak Basque," I said. "Except when he's arguing with you."

"*Ba,*" Aitatxi dug the tip of his walking stick into the dirt. "*Aitain bihotza*—father's heart, it no want a remember Euskara now."

"How come?"

"*Zure aita,* he think only of what coming and forget what already come."

"What's wrong with that?" I said. "I mean, the past was when Mom died. Why wouldn't Dad want to forget it?"

"It also when you born," Aitatxi said. "*Ttipia eta itsusia. Bildotza gaixua.*"

I started to smile at the familiar description of me at my birth, but then I had a thought that made my stomach knot up. Maybe that was what I was to Dad—a piece of the past. Something to be forgotten. Maybe that was why he was always going out of town for work.

"*Ene semea,*" Aitatxi said, "my son, he no remember that with no yesterday they no tomorrow."

"Teach me," I said.

"*Zer?*"

"Basque," I said.

"Say please," Aitatxi said.

"Please."

"In Euskara."

"*Plazer baduzu,*" I said, surprised at the words that came out of my mouth.

"*Untxa,*" Aitatxi smiled. "*Zure bihotza,* it remember."

ten | hamar

For the next couple of hours, Aitatxi taught me both Basque and shepherding.

"*Eguzkia,*" Aitatxi said as he pointed up at the sun.

I repeated the word. "A-goos-key-uh."

"Come *gau*—night," Aitatxi said. "*Eguzkia,* he trade places with wife, *illargia*—moon."

"Ill-r-g—doesn't Basque have any easy words?"

"*Ba.*"

"Great."

In English, Aitatxi told me how "we" needed to keep the sheep close together.

"So sheeps, they one big ball of wool," Aitatxi said.

The dogs pretty much took care of this by constantly circling the flock. Aitatxi's job, and now mine, was to make sure none of the sheep broke away from the flock and wandered off into the desert.

"Sheeps, they go every way *baina* right way you let them," Aitatxi said.

Aitatxi told me about the danger of "jumping" cholla

cactus that grew like small, gnarled trees over the sand. "Sheeps, they get in cactus we big time trouble. Thorns, they like fishhooks. I hate those."

"Hate, that big word," I said. "Really two words—hat with the e."

"*Ba, gaixua,* and in desert, I no like both."

Aitatxi pointed with his walking stick at some black vultures circling in the distance. "Black bird, they smell death. We no want them fly over *gure ardiak*—our sheeps."

Whenever a sheep ran off from the main flock, Aitatxi would tell me what to say to Atarrabi and Mikelats to get it back. I tried to say the words just like Aitatxi did, but sometimes it was like my mouth was full of marbles. When that happened, the dogs turned toward me with raised ears and say-what? looks on their faces. "*Berriz,*" Aitatxi would say to me, and with his help I'd repeat the words and get the dogs going.

Even though I suspected I was tricked into learning both shepherding and Basque by Aitatxi, I didn't mind. I liked the feeling of being in control for a change. And when I got the words Aitatxi told me right and the dogs did exactly what I wanted, he would say, "*Untxa*" and I'd find myself unable to stop grinning.

There was another reason I liked saying the Basque words Aitatxi taught me. Even though most of the words came out sounding nothing like Aitatxi's, some, like "*haugi hunat*"—come here, and "*guazen fite*"—go quickly, rolled off my tongue as if I'd said them a hundred times. It was like remembering something I didn't know I knew—or someone. I heard my mother's voice as I spoke the same words she must have said to me as a baby. And while I still couldn't put together a solid picture of my mother in my head, at least now I knew what she sounded like.

The desert in front of us remained brown, with the only really green patches coming from some bushes with tiny, shiny leaves. The hotter it got, the greener the bushes looked. And while the sheep nibbled at any plant that poked up through the sand, including the cholla, they stayed away from the shiny bushes. I found out why when I pulled off a handful of leaves from one of the bushes. The leaves stuck to my fingers like they were coated in honey. But when I raised the leaves to my nose, it wasn't sweet honey I smelled but something like garlic dipped in vinegar. I sneezed. I wiped the leaves off on my pants, but even when they were gone the smell hung on my skin.

"It creosote," Aitatxi said, and told me that after a rain the whole desert smelled of the plant. "Only no so *fiera*—strong. Only tickle nose, make clear head. Good when you got cold."

I questioned Aitatxi about everything we passed and soon learned that what he knew about the desert was limited to things that he could use and things that caused him problems. Everything else Aitatxi dismissed with a shrug and "I no like."

Quail were good to eat. Hawks were just big birds that flew by. Coyotes were Deabrua's—the devil's children and had to be watched for. Jackrabbits tasted like "bottom of shoe" and made the "*txakurrak* forget about sheeps." And snakes, rattlers especially, were all "thing you no want a wake up in bedroll next you."

As the day wore on, my string of questions began to break apart. Aitatxi's answers grew short, usually no more than a word or two—"no eat" or "no know." The sun seemed hotter and closer than it was the day before, and I was glad for Oxea's beret. Aitatxi didn't say anything when he saw me wearing it. He just nodded and took a drink of wine from his *zakua*.

The hotter the day got, the more watery the horizon became. After a while, it was like we were walking toward a rolling line of waves. Only we never reached the waves. Like the tide going out, the water retreated before us. Cactus stuck up like coral from the sand. And for the first time, the stuff I learned in school about the desert once being underwater didn't seem like something our science teacher, Mr. Schmidt, made up.

The sheep moved forward in a single dusty bunch of wool. Or they seemed to at first. But as I watched the flock, I began to pick out individual sheep from the group. A fat sheep in the middle that I named Rollo never seemed to be going the right way and bounced off the sheep on either side of him whenever the flock changed direction. A sheep near the back of the flock, Snoopy, was always jumping up and bleating as if sure he was missing something fun going on up front. And then there was Gaixua. He was at the very back of the flock. Gaixua was shorter than the other sheep and looked like he hadn't had a good meal in a while. Atarrabi and Mikelats were always nipping at him to catch up. As the sun grew whiter with heat, I worried a lot about Gaixua.

Sometime in the afternoon, after a walking lunch of bread and cheese and warm water from my *zakua,* I heard Aitatxi's footsteps stop.

"*Nola?*" he said. "How is?"

I was walking beside him with my head down. I'd pushed my beret forward to protect my face from the sun and could only see a small spot of desert directly in front of me. But when Aitatxi stopped, I looked up and saw that the rolling waves had turned green.

Aitatxi took off his beret. He scratched the top of his head and leaned forward.

"*Nola?*" Aitatxi said again as he rubbed his eyes with his beret.

Like Aitatxi, I might have thought what I was seeing was a mirage if it hadn't been for the small white vehicles sailing over the green waves.

"It's a golf course."

"Sure, no, I know is golf course," Aitatxi said. "*Baina* I no know why golf course here."

"You haven't been this way in a while, Aitatxi. Things change."

He let out a grunt of disgust and jammed his walking stick into the sand.

"It's no big deal," I said.

Aitatxi stood there glaring at the line of green in our path.

"*Mendia heltzen da urratz bat aldian.*"

"What does that mean?"

But Aitatxi wouldn't say. He just replaced his beret on his head and clicked his tongue.

"We can go around it," I said.

"*Ez, ez, guazen,*" Aitatxi said. "We go."

Then he pulled his walking stick out of the ground and started toward the golf course.

"But sheep aren't allowed on a golf course," was all I could think to say as I followed after him.

"Golf course no should be allow in desert," Aitatxi said, swinging his walking stick in front of him and looking just like the picture of Moses with his staff in our Bible at home. Only Aitatxi wasn't going to part the Red Sea, but a green one.

eleven | hamaika

The minute we stepped onto the golf course's grass, the sheep started grazing, and not even Atarrabi and Mikelats could get them moving again. And moving was what I wanted to do. If I was lucky, I could get Aitatxi and his sheep across the golf course without being seen. I thought this was possible because most of the course's holes, along with a building that I figured was the pro shop, were well off to the right. Only a couple of holes reached out into the desert in front of us. How hard could cutting across two fairways be?

"*Ardiak igorri,*" I yelled at Atarrabi and Mikelats. "Sheep forward." And both of the panting dogs took time out from barking and running around the sheep to give me looks that said, "Why don't you come back here and give it a go your-self, big mouth?"

I was thinking I might just have to do that when Aitatxi took control. He raised his walking stick and called out in-structions to Atarrabi and Mikelats, and, like he was the Pied Piper, the sheep began to follow him across the first fairway. As he went, Aitatxi started into his version of Wayne Newton's "Daddy, Don't You Walk So Fast."

"Daddy no you *ardiak ez dute behar hainfite joan,*" Aitatxi sang. "Daddy no you sheeps should go so fast."

I didn't even bother commenting on his singing. All I wanted was to get across the golf course without getting caught. I imagined how Aitatxi, in broken English, would explain to a head pro dressed in flowered pants and an Izod shirt what a flock of sheep was doing on his golf course—"Sure, no, grass is for eating by sheeps and no for hitting ball on."

And then I thought, who cares? So what if Aitatxi got caught? What was I worried about? After all, Aitatxi was the adult. He was the one who would be in trouble. Me, I was just a kid.

I grinned as Aitatxi and the sheep tromped through a sand trap. Somebody was going to need to rake that big time. Dad had taken me out to play on the public course by our house a couple of times, but I didn't like it. Golf was full of too many don'ts: don't talk when someone is putting, don't hit out of turn, don't swing until the other golfers are out of the way, don't drive the cart up on the green, and, an unsaid don't—don't run a flock of sheep through a sand trap. I followed after Aitatxi and the sheep.

The sheep were *baa*ing and Aitatxi was singing and the whole thing was kind of cool. I mean, not many people could say they drove the eighteenth fairway with thirty-two sheep instead of a three-wood. The kids at school would laugh when I told them abou—I stopped midstep with my right foot hanging in the air as I heard Rich say, "Hey, Mathieu, what kind of balls do sheep use, Titleist or Maxfli?" And the kids pointing at me and calling me sheep-boy. Things were bad enough with me being the bass-boy from Eden. I didn't need to give the kids at school more ammo to humiliate me with.

I started walking again, faster now. I had to keep Aitatxi and the sheep going. If we got caught on the golf course, the newspaper would run a story about it, and Ms. Helm would cut out the article and put it on the bulletin board, and there would be a picture—one of me and Aitatxi wearing matching berets and surrounded by sheep. No, no, no. I broke into a jog.

"*Joaiten gira! Guazen fite!*" I yelled at Aitatxi and the sheep. "Let's go! Hurry up!"

Aitatxi looked at me, seemingly pleased at my sudden burst of enthusiasm, and said, "*Orai* you acting like *artzaina, gaixua.*"

There were no golfers in sight as we moved onto the second fairway. I could see the brown desert beyond the white out-of-bounds stakes at the grass's edge. I took a deep breath. We were going to make it. Then Aitatxi and the flock suddenly stopped, and I turned to see the sheep line up along the edge of the hole's lake and start to drink. Aitatxi stood watching over the sheep with Atarrabi and Mikelats lying at his feet.

"*Guazen!*" I said.

"*Ez, gaixua,* sheeps need *ura.*"

"I thought you said sheep didn't drink that much."

"Good drink after meal, always nice thing," Aitatxi said.

"We've got to go now."

"*Zendako?*" Aitatxi said. "Why?"

"We don't have time."

"We got time for drink. Sure, no, we near *isiliko* trail, *gaixua.* No worry, we no get this day, *baina* by next day morning, we there."

"You don't understand, Aitatxi," I said. "We have to—"

And that was when the four women drove their golf carts into Aitatxi's sheep.

The women were talking and not paying attention as they came around the far side of the lake. They must have been trusting in the cart path to lead them safely to the next tee box. I could have told them that no path was really safe—especially one my *aitatxi* was on.

The women didn't even look up until their carts were well into the flock. Even then I heard one woman saying, "And Mary, I swear he had been smo—" Then she screamed, and the flock exploded like a cherry bomb. The sheep jumped into the air as if a coyote was among them. The first cart swerved to miss the sheep and ended up in the lake. The second cart managed to stay out of the water, but to do it the woman driving had to spin the cart in a 360, which sent her passenger tumbling onto the grass. When the woman who was thrown from the cart sat up, she said, "What the hell is going on?"

I couldn't breathe. I was doomed. And it wasn't over yet.

Mikelats jumped on top of the cart in the water and started barking. Atarrabi followed him, only instead of barking, he chose to howl. And, rising up through the dogs' barking and howling and the bleating of sheep were the screams of the woman in the passenger seat of the cart in the lake. Somehow Gaixua had ended up on her lap. The woman didn't stop screaming until the cart's driver said, "Shut up, Linda. It's only a sheep."

I felt like crying as I looked over at Aitatxi, who just shook his head and said, "Ladies drivers."

Aitatxi walked over and helped up the woman on the grass as I ran to the cart in the lake.

"Atarrabi, Mikelats, *isilik*," I said. "Be quiet. *Haugi hunat.* Come here."

The dogs jumped off the cart's roof. I waded into the two-foot-deep water and kept my eyes down as I lifted Gaixua off the woman's lap. I set Gaixua on dry land. The sheep took a wobbly step, then sat down on the grass. He seemed to be as shaken up by what had happened as the woman was.

Aitatxi went to the driver's side of the cart.

"*Pardone,* ladies," Aitatxi said. "*Baina* sheep, how can you do?"

Well, the woman who was driving thought of something she could do. She took the end of the putter she was holding and popped Aitatxi in the middle of his forehead. Aitatxi stumbled back.

"Hey!" I yanked the woman's putter from her hand and threw it into the lake.

"Asshole," the woman said and put the cart into reverse. With a spray of mud and water, she backed out of the lake. "I'm reporting you to the pro shop," she yelled at Aitatxi, who was still standing in the water rubbing his head. Then she added, "Come on, Connie," to the woman driving the other cart and sped away.

I waded over to Aitatxi and helped him out of the lake.

"I can't believe that old bat hit you."

"Lady upset," Aitatxi said as he removed his hand from his head. I saw he was bleeding from the cut there.

"That bitc—"

"Gaixua, you no say—they ladies."

"Crazy ladies," I said.

"No dressed good ladies," Aitatxi said.

"Wet ladies."

"Who no like sheeps." Aitatxi grinned.

I started to laugh as I heard, "Excuse me."

Aitatxi and I turned around to see the woman who had

been driving the other cart standing there. Her cart was parked ten yards away. The passenger who'd been thrown out sat inside rubbing her rear.

"Oh," the woman said to Aitatxi, "you're hurt."

Her skin was the color of dark chocolate and looked like it needed a good ironing.

"It nothing," Aitatxi said, even as he squeezed his eyes closed, leaned his head forward, and then flinched as he lightly touched the cut with his finger.

"Sit down." The woman pulled a handkerchief out of her pocket. "Mary's got to learn to control that temper of hers."

Aitatxi sat on the grass and removed his beret. Then as the woman examined the cut on his head, he gave me a wink. I shook my head. The old faker.

"I'm Connie Bart," the woman said after she'd cleaned the blood away from the cut.

"Mathieu Etcheberri." Aitatxi took her hand and gave a little bow to her the same way he'd done to my teacher, Ms. Helm.

"I know," Connie said. "I read about you in the morning paper. You and your grandson are quite the outlaws."

"The newspaper?" I said.

Connie nodded. "Front page."

"Oh, my God."

Headlines flashed through my head: MATT ECHBAR ARRESTED FOR SHEEP STAMPEDE and LOCAL BOY TO DO TIME FOR DISOBEYING FATHER.

"Where are you taking the sheep?" Connie asked. Her teeth had yellow stripes on them.

"We could tell you," I said, "but then we'd have to kill you."

Connie laughed. Aitatxi glared at me.

"I understand," Connie said. "You need to keep your

destination secret. It must be exciting to have an adventure like this at your age."

"I no so old," Aitatxi growled.

"Oh," Connie said, "I meant your grandson. He's lucky to have a grandfather like you."

"Lucky," Aitatxi said. "Listen that, *gaixua*. You lucky."

"Great."

"You enjoy this, young man," Connie said. "All my grandchildren live in Ohio, and I only get to see them on holidays."

"No is right," Aitatxi said.

"It's my own fault," Connie said. "I thought sunshine and golf would be enough in my retirement. But it isn't, is it?"

Connie gazed off across the lake as if looking at something on the other side, and I saw how her red lipstick was clumped up on the corners of her mouth.

Aitatxi again took her hand, and this time he kissed it.

"Every adventure, it need beautiful lady," he said.

Connie looked down at where Aitatxi kissed her hand. There were tears in her eyes.

"I'm sorry your son did this to you," Connie said. "He had no right to sell your sheep."

"He nice boy," Aitatxi said. "He only forget he my boy."

"They always do," Connie said. "You better get moving before Mary shows up with the posse."

Aitatxi walked over to Atarrabi and Mikelats. And while he and the dogs gathered up the sheep, Connie turned to me. "Your father's worried about you."

"What? How do yo—"

"They had a quote from him in the newspaper article," Connie said. "He said you've always been a good boy."

A good boy? Sure, no. I was a good boy who started fires and stole sheep and couldn't be trusted to look after his *aitatxi*.

"Would you like to send him a message?" Connie pulled a scorecard and pencil out of her pants pocket. "Just write down what you want to say and your phone number. Don't worry, I'll wait until you've made a clean getaway before I call him."

I took the scorecard and pencil from Connie. I looked over at Aitatxi splashing along the edge of the lake as he drove the last of the sheep from the water. If he wasn't my *aitatxi*, I might have laughed at the old guy knee-deep in water, wearing an oversized black jacket and a beret lying flat on top of his head. But he was my *aitatxi*. And Dad had asked me to look after him. So far, nothing really bad had happened. But what if something did? What if Aitatxi got hurt? Good boys did what their fathers said.

I wrote my phone number on the back of the scorecard and the words "Bradshaw's—*etxola*—secret trail" and handed the card back to Connie.

"Let's go, Connie," the woman in the cart called.

"Hold on half a sec." Connie ran over to the cart. She grabbed a couple of bags out of the cart as the other woman said, "But I'm hungry." When Aitatxi walked up, Connie handed us each a sandwich.

"*Mil esker*," Aitatxi said.

"Yeah, thanks." I hungrily unwrapped my sandwich.

"Mind if I take a picture of you two outlaws?" Connie held up a small camera.

"Sure, no," Aitatxi said and threw an arm around my shoulder. Before I could argue, he pulled me close to him and said, "*Zuretako hauda*."

Connie snapped the picture, and I pulled myself free from his grasp.

"We go *orai,*" Aitatxi said.

"Good luck," Connie said.

"*Izan untxa,*" Aitatxi said. "Be well."

When we were out of earshot, Aitatxi poked me with his walking stick. "You listen, *gaixua?* We outlaws. Ladies love outlaws."

"Yeah, yeah." I took a bite of my sandwich. Unlike Aitatxi's hard sourdough that I had to chip away at with my front teeth, I bit through the white bread like it was air. The bread dissolved in my mouth. Beneath it was salty ham. I grinned as I chewed the rubbery meat and felt the processed cheese slick on my tongue. I licked mustard from my lips and swallowed. Finally, real food.

"Are you going to eat all your sandwich?" I said. "Because if you're no—"

"I must," Aitatxi said. "It of *bihotza*—heart."

"No, it's ham and cheese," I said.

When we reached the end of the second fairway, Aitatxi looked back. Connie was still standing there watching us. Aitatxi raised his beret into the air and waved to her. Connie held up her white golf glove and waved back.

"Oh, brother," I said.

"*Isilik,*" Aitatxi said. "Be quiet."

As I watched Aitatxi and Connie waving to each other across the fairway, I knew I'd done the right thing by letting Dad know where we were going. Aitatxi had had his adventure, complete with a beautiful lady . . . or at least Connie. Now was it was time to go home.

I figured once Connie called Dad, he'd tell the police where Aitatxi was taking the sheep. By this afternoon, Dad and the police would drive up to the *etxola* on the road Oxea and Aitatxi always used. From there, it was just a matter of backtracking the trail we were on until they found us. I'd be sleeping in my own bed that night.

"*Joaiten gira,*" Aitatxi said as he turned away from the golf course and led me back into the desert.

twelve | hamabi

By late afternoon, Aitatxi and I were still outlaws. I regularly searched the horizon for sunlight reflecting off approaching squad cars, but nothing broke up the wavy brown desert. As we walked, I realized the one flaw in my plan for being captured was Aitatxi's "secret trail." Did Dad know about the trail? Aitatxi said he did . . . kind of—sure, no. Was there really even a trail? Maybe Aitatxi was making the whole thing up. Still, I was positive Dad would find us once he knew we were headed to the *etxola*—secret trail or not.

I decided to stop worrying about Dad and start worrying about what I was going to say to Aitatxi when the police surrounded us. Confessing that I'd squealed on him was not an option. I planned on acting all disappointed, like I wanted to keep walking on and on through the desert with a bunch of stinking sheep for the rest of my life. Aitatxi didn't need to know I'd ratted him out. Even if I did it for his own good. I mean, I was looking out for him. Like Dad told me to do. Aitatxi was just too old for a sheep drive.

Only right then, Aitatxi didn't look too old. He was practically running forward, and I had to quicken my pace to keep up with him.

Now that Atarrabi and Mikelats had the flock thing down, all Aitatxi and I did was walk behind the sheep and keep a lookout for strays—which was usually Gaixua; he kept falling behind. My legs weren't as sore as they had been in the morning. And though I did wish I'd looked for a water fountain back at the golf course, Aitatxi let me take regular drinks from my *zakua.*

"Tomorrow day, we find Oxea's *iturritza,*" Aitatxi said. "It water so clear you see there God."

Not that I knew what God was doing in water or for that matter what God looked like. To me, God was like the sun. I could feel the warmth coming from him, but he was too far away to see clearly and too bright to look at for long. Which was fine with me. I mean, God knew everything that I thought and did. EVERYTHING. For someone who had trouble "sharing" even the little things of everyday life, "everything" was just too big for me to handle. And while I couldn't picture God, right then I knew he was scowling down at me.

"This good thing," Aitatxi said, "we together like this. We got good adventure, sure, no, *gaixua.*"

I kept my eyes on the ground in front of me and nodded.

"Two days more," Aitatxi said, "we come at *etxola.*"

Dad was probably there right now.

Clouds moved across the sky to block out the sun and gave us a little relief from the heat. And while it was still hot, I could no longer actually feel my skin cooking. Slowly the desert started to change. New bushes showed up among the creosote. They were taller and grew up over my head and were covered with red berries.

"They small-apple bush," Aitatxi said. But when I ate one of the "small apples" it tasted like a rotten potato.

"No for eat, *gaixua,*" Aitatxi said. "*Baina* Oxea, he make into good drink. Like *arno zuria*—white wine, only no make head fuzzy."

Scattered among the small-apple bushes were a few of what Aitatxi called "armored trees."

"They think maybe they cactus." Aitatxi used the tip of his walking stick to touch a two-inch thorn on one of the trees. "You no want a get fight with thems."

And there were other cactus, besides chollas, now. Some, like barrel cactus and saguaro, I knew from landscaped yards in Phoenix. Others I'd never seen before. There were thin cactus with tentacle-like arms reaching toward the sky and topped with orange flowers. And short cactus with flat, wide pads that looked like beavers' tails, only with spikes. To pass the time, I asked Aitatxi the name of every new cactus I saw. But unless the cactus could be eaten, Aitatxi said, "No thing *baina* stickers. I try eat fruit one time, *txarra da*—it no so good."

Lizards, some as tiny as my little finger and others as thick as my arm, raced from the shade of one cactus to the next. Lines of bobbing quail cut across our path, and when we got too close, the birds took off in low flight for about ten yards and then hit the ground running. Other birds jumped and flew within the limbs of the armored trees. The chirping and whistling seemed to make the trees sing. A lone roadrunner sprinted right through the middle of the flock. Snoopy jumped straight into the air as the bird passed. Aitatxi guided the sheep through a minefield of red-ant hills. The ants blanketed the ground, their red bodies moving like lava over the sand. I decided that ants ruled the desert, through numbers alone.

The desert was supposed to be a place of death. At least that is what I'd been taught. But if that was true, there sure was a lot of living going on among the dead.

The sun was falling toward the horizon when the sand we were walking on grew rough with broken stones. We'd been slowly going uphill ever since we left the golf course. And when I looked back the way we'd come, I saw the slope covered with washes, one trailing into the other. The washes worked their way down into the valley below. In one of those washes I spotted a coyote.

The coyote's nose was to the ground. He worked it from side to side as he followed our path. The smell of sheep must have been like a paved highway of stink leading the coyote right to us.

I picked up a rock and threw it down the slope in the direction of the coyote. It hit off a boulder with a clank. The coyote looked up at the sound. For a moment our eyes met. Then the coyote flicked his nose at me as if saying, "Fine, you caught me this time, but I'll be back," and slipped into the bushes.

Aitatxi called to me to catch up, and as I ran to him, the wind filled my ears like the rush of water. I fell into step with Aitatxi and was about to tell him how the coyote was following us, but before I could, he said, "We need talk."

Aitatxi's beret was pushed back on his head, and he had both his hands on his walking stick.

"What is it?" I said.

Aitatxi didn't look at me. Instead he kept his eyes down and wrinkled up his lips like there was something sour-tasting in his mouth. And I knew what that sour taste was—me. Aitatxi must have figured out what I'd done. But how? He hadn't seen what I wrote on the golf card, and I'd have heard if Connie had told him. He couldn't know. Still, he was Aitatxi—and he seemed to always know a heck of a lot more than I thought he did. My stomach knotted up with guilt. It was one thing to be a stool pigeon; it was another thing to get caught at it.

"Let me explai—"

"No explain here," Aitatxi said. "It just time."

"Time?"

"Time you find you-self nice wife."

"Huh?"

"You wait more, it past late."

"But I'm only thirteen."

"Best time get seeing." Aitatxi pointed at me with the tip of his walking stick. "I you age first time see *zure amatxi.*"

"You married Amatxi when she was only thirteen?"

"Sure, no, you got ears. I say 'see,' no 'marry.' Amatxi, she at church, I see."

Aitatxi used his walking stick to nudge Gaixua to keep up with the flock.

"What did you say to her?"

"Uh, you no listen. I no 'say,' I 'see.'"

"Fine, then what did you say to Amatxi when you did 'say' to her?"

"Happy birthday," Aitatxi said like he had answered the winning question on a game show.

"You said that to her after church?"

"*Zer* church? She at *pelote* match. I get her glass wine—ladies like *arno zuria.*"

"But she was only thirteen," I said.

"Who say that?"

"You did."

"Sure, no, Amatxi, she turn eighteen year that day."

I pushed my beret up on my head to match Aitatxi's.

"Okay," I said, "let's start over. You saw Amatxi when she was thirteen in church."

"*Ba.*"

"But the first time you talked to her was on her birthday at a *pelote* match when she turned eighteen."

"*Untxa,*" Aitatxi said. "*Orai* you listening."

"Yeah, I listening—that's five years from when you saw her to when you talked to her."

"Sure, no." Aitatxi shook his head apologetically. "I hurry bit. *Baina* I could no wait more."

"I think you waited lon—"

"*Beha zazu,*" Aitatxi said. "See you." He came to a stop and pointed at a line of buildings in the distance. "*Zer da?*"

"Houses, I think," I said.

"*Zer dira hemengo etxeak?*" Aitatxi said. "How houses doing here?"

"It's a housing development."

Aitatxi started walking again, and I followed. As we got closer, I could see that the houses were built close together, their walls almost touching. Red-brick chimneys stuck up like fingers pointing toward the sky. But none of the houses were complete. Through the wooden frames of the first row of houses, I saw more unfinished houses beyond.

"How houses doing this place?"

"I guess people want to live here."

Aitatxi stopped again and scowled at the houses as if that would make them go away. Atarrabi and Mikelats held the sheep together as they waited for Aitatxi to tell them what to do.

"First golf course, *orai* houses," Aitatxi said. "I no like. How next? Disneyland?"

"They're just houses."

"They no belong here."

"Kind of like sheep in the desert," I said. And Aitatxi looked at me with eyes like coals. I could see the muscles of his jaw working beneath his gray whiskers as if he was chewing up my words. I wished I'd kept my mouth shut.

"We go through *prishazite,*" Aitatxi said. "Quickly."

"After what happened at the golf course, maybe we should go around the houses," I said.

"*Ez,*" Aitatxi said. "No can go around. They no only houses."

"Of course they are."

"No you see, *gaixua?*" Aitatxi said. "Houses, they death."

"What are you talking about?"

But Aitatxi wouldn't say anymore. Not in English anyway.

"*Xagi xagi*—keep going. *Zaza zuzen zuzena,*" he said to Atarrabi and Mikelats. "Go straight, right now."

The dogs got the sheep moving again. And as we walked, Aitatxi kept his head down. His lips were moving, and I heard whispered words in Basque repeated over and over. After a moment, I realized Aitatxi was praying. Maybe to Oxea, thinking about his brother in these houses of death. Or maybe to God, asking for the strength to finish his journey. Or maybe, like me, he was praying that Dad would be inside one of the unfinished houses waiting to take us home.

thirteen | hamahiru

The setting sun turned the world from gray to red as we approached the first row of houses. There was no glass in any of the windows, and tumbleweeds filled the empty doorways.

"*Guazen fite,*" Aitatxi said. "Go quickly."

"What's the hurry? There's no one here."

"We go." Aitatxi raised his walking stick to drive the sheep forward.

The houses were so close to each other, it was easier to go through their unfinished frames than between them. We moved past empty swimming pools lined with cracks. Wires and pipes stuck out from the pools' walls.

"Why didn't they finish them?" I said as we stepped onto the cement floor of one of the houses. I picked up a piece of broken board and held it up. "Did something happen?"

"Mamu happen," Aitatxi said.

"The Mamu?" I dropped the board onto the cement.

"*Guazen.*" Aitatxi cut through a house that was more complete than the rest, with solid walls and the beginning of a roof. Something darted past a doorway off to my right. My head swung around expecting to see a long hairy arm, but instead I spotted a fat rear end and heard a long *baaaaa.*

It was Rollo.

Aitatxi heard the sheep as well and said, "You get" and waved his walking stick toward where the bleating came from. "Go *fite*—fast." And before I could tell him to send one of the dogs, Aitatxi was out the back doorway. I saw him scramble over a half-built wall as he followed the rest of the flock into the next house.

Great. I was left to get the sheep on my own. Not that finding Rollo was that big a deal. Not usually, anyway. Only here . . . Why did Aitatxi have to bring up the Mamu? The day's light was almost gone. It could turn to night at any moment. And then where would I be? Alone, walking in the dark with the Mamu. No thanks. I needed to find Rollo fast.

"Rollo!"

Images of the Mamu's scarred face floated through my head as long shadows slipped into the house. I moved toward the doorway Rollo had passed by. A startled bird flew overhead. My heart matched the quick beats of its wings.

"Rollo," I called again—not that calling him was any good. He didn't know I'd named him Rollo. Still, the sound of my own voice made me feel less alone.

I sneezed and used the back of my arm to wipe my nose. Which didn't help, since a layer of dust covered my skin. I sneezed again. Dust was everywhere. It was like I was inside some Egyptian tomb.

I hurried after Rollo, keeping my focus on finding the sheep and getting out of there. That is, until I heard something move—something big—in the next room. I held my breath and listened. But there was only the barking of Atarrabi and Mikelats. The dogs sounded far away.

"Don't be such a baby," I told myself and stepped into the room. It was large, like a cave, and the lost sheep wasn't in it. The only other door in the room was on the far side. Rollo must have gone that way.

"Get out here, you stupid sheep." I was angry now as well as scared. I rushed across the room and in doing so almost fell in the hole that was cut in the middle of the floor. My foot was halfway over the edge before I realized it was there. I jumped to the side to keep from falling in.

"Geez!"

I gazed into the manhole-size opening. Why would anyone put a hole in the middle of a room? I peered into the darkness. How deep was it? Had Rollo fallen in the hole? I leaned over to get a better look. Cool air rose up over my face. It smelled stale, like a room that hadn't been opened for a long time. And I wasn't thinking months but years. There was no sound.

Since I couldn't see the hole's bottom, I decided to spit and then listen for it to splat against something solid. Only it never did.

"Deep hole." My words were repeated as they fell. "Cool."

"Cool, cool, cool, cool," echoed back from the depths of the hole.

I leaned over further to hear better. Smiled. This was fun. I was about to say another word, and for some reason "jump" came to mind. But before I could get the word out, something grabbed me. My arms pinwheeled. I lost my balance. I was falling into the hole. Then Aitatxi jerked me back. His hand was on my shoulder and the lost Rollo was beside him. I had that foggy feeling of having just woken up. But I hadn't been asleep.

"*Gaixua*, we go," Aitatxi said and turned and walked out of the room. I followed, only pausing for a moment at the doorway to look back. The hole was gone. Or at least I couldn't see it now, the opening again lost in the room's shadows. I hurried after Aitatxi.

Outside I was surprised by how much daylight there still was. Inside the house, the day had seemed to be slipping into night. But now, though there wasn't a lot of light left, there was enough to see the road we stood on. It dead-ended in front of the unfinished houses. There, a faded sign read: WARREN HOMES. HAPPINESS STARTING IN THE LOW 60S.

In the other direction the road ran back through the desert toward Phoenix. The lights at the outskirts of the city were blinking on, and I wished I was there, surrounded by people, in my house, turning on my desk lamp, waiting for Dad to come up and say good night.

But I wasn't. I was here with Aitatxi and his sheep and a bunch of dead houses. I was about to ask Aitatxi what the Mamu had to do with the houses when three boys on bikes rode up.

"There you are," the biggest of the three boys said.

He rode a Schwinn Pea Picker. The very bike I wanted for my birthday last year—still wanted. On my wall at home there was an article from a magazine telling all about the bike. The Pea Picker was one of Schwinn's Stingray series of muscle bikes—just the sound of that made me feel tough. The green bike came with a banana seat, monkey handlebars, an under-sized front tire, and a five-speed stick shift on the top tube. No boy couldn't want that bike. It was killer. I'd even told that to Aitatxi, but he still gave me a sheep instead.

"We've been waiting for you forever," the boy on "my" bike said. He looked about the same age as me. Freckles covered his face.

The sheep moved around and between the bikes until the boys were in the middle of the flock.

"Yeah," the skinny boy said. He was riding a yellow Lemon Peeler. "We thought the cops nailed you." His head was shaved.

The littlest boy, whose bike was ten different colors and looked like it was made of used parts, nodded his head and said, "In jail."

"What are you talking about?" I said,

"It's all over the news," the freckle-faced boy said.

"How you stole the sheep," the skinny boy said.

"In jail," the littlest boy said again as he petted Gaixua, who was chewing on the edge of his shirt.

"The woman from the golf course told the police you were going to the Estrellas," the freckle-faced boy said. He looked at Aitatxi. "She was crying when she said how you swore her to secrecy and how she was only spilling the beans because she cared."

"She great lady," Aitatxi said.

Great? Right then, the only thing I thought was "great" about Connie was her acting ability. She lied to the police and told them we were headed in the opposite direction than we were. No wonder we hadn't seen any sign of pursuit. I hoped she got jail time when Dad set the police straight. But why hadn't he done that already? Maybe Connie never called him. But why bother telling me she was going to call Dad if she didn't mean to? Dad must not have made it back from Colorado yet. Once he got home, this whole thing would be over. Still, that meant another night of Aitatxi and his sheep and no Dad.

"But I knew you'd come this way," the skinny boy said.

"I knew," the freckle-faced boy said.

"How?" I said.

"I just drew a line on the map from the golf course to the nearest mountains," the freckle-faced boy said.

"The Bradshaws are lots closer than the Estrellas," the skinny boy said.

Kids could find us, no problem. But the police, forget it. The sheep began to lie down on the road, and Atarrabi and Mikelats whined.

"We near *isileko* trail," Aitatxi said. "*Baina* no find in night."

"What are we going to do?" I said.

Aitatxi looked back at the empty houses behind us. The freckle-faced boy saw him and said, "That's no good. The police are sure to look there sooner or later."

"Besides, that place is haunted," the skinny boy said.

"Ghosts," the littlest boy said.

"Shut up," the freckle-faced boy said.

"*Baina* we must go desert," Aitatxi said.

"No, you don't," the skinny boy said.

"We've got the perfect hideout for you," the freckle-faced boy said.

"Perfect," the littlest boy said.

"Yeah, c'mon," the skinny boy said.

The three boys pushed their way through the sheep and started pedaling away down the road.

"It's not too far," the freckle-faced boy yelled back at us.

"Follow the road," the skinny boy said.

"Follow the road," the littlest boy repeated.

As we watched them ride away, I said, "What are we going to do?"

"*Hortik bidea,*" Aitatxi said. "Follow road."

Atarrabi and Mikelats went to work, and soon Aitatxi and the flock and I were all heading down the road after the boys and back toward the twinkling lights of the city.

fourteen | hamalau

The road led to Christmas Town.

The place was abandoned and now just an empty cement square without a roof. A peeling sign said: SANTA LIVES IN THE DESERT. There were wood cutouts of an unpainted sled and a ten-foot-tall headless Santa in front of the building. As we moved the sheep inside, the freckle-faced boy told us that they had stopped working on Christmas Town five years ago when the housing development went bust.

"They want to turn it into an adult bookstore," the skinny boy said.

"My mom says she'll burn the place down if they try that," the freckle-faced boy said.

"My dad said there's no reason adults shouldn't have their own bookstore to get good reading material," the skinny boy said.

"You're a knucklehead," the freckle-faced boy said. Then he turned to Aitatxi and said, "You'll be safe here. No one comes near this place since all the trouble."

"A group of moms came out and knocked Santa's head off," the skinny boy said.

"Knocked Santa's head off," the littlest boy said.

"We got to go now," the freckle-faced boy said. "It's time for dinner."

"But we'll come back in the morning," the skinny boy said. "You like donuts?"

"Chocolate glazed," Aitatxi said.

"Is there any other kind?" the freckle-faced boy said.

As the boys rode their bikes out of the empty store, Aitatxi waved. "*Mil esker, izan untxa*—be well."

"They don't speak Euskara, Aitatxi," I said.

"They know with *bihotzak*—hearts," Aitatxi said. "*Orai*, get rope, we make pen for sheeps."

While I got the rope from my pack, Aitatxi had Atarrabi and Mikelats work the sheep into a corner of the building. We then tied the rope to the electrical wires that dangled out of the cement walls and penned in the sheep.

After that, Aitatxi sent me to find some wood for a fire. Around the back of the building, I found a pile of wooden cutout elves. The elves were all in different poses of toy making. I also found a stack of old magazines. Most of them had Camaros and Chevy Supersports on their covers. But I did find a copy of a *Boys' Life* with an article in it titled "Surviving the Wild: Ten Knots You Need to Know" and an October issue of *Playboy*, only all the pictures were ripped out. I broke up a couple of elves and carried the pieces, along with the magazines—minus the *Playboy*—inside.

Aitatxi used the magazines to start a fire on the cement floor. I watched the flames rise into a sky full of stars. Aitatxi got out the sheep's milk cheese and sourdough bread. And even though I was sick of both, I ate what he gave me greedily.

I couldn't remember ever being so hungry. While we ate, Aitatxi hummed, and for once it was a song I didn't recognize from the radio.

"What song is that?"

"It my song," Aitatxi said.

"You wrote a song?"

"No worry, *gaixua*, you in my song."

"Let me guess—it's about a boy who was was born *ttipia eta itsusia* and goes on a sheeps drive in the desert," I said.

"*Ez, baina* that good," Aitatxi said. "My song about city boy, he learn how *mendia heltzen da urratz bat aldian.*"

"What's that mean?"

"You maybe learn tomorrow day," Aitatxi said. "*Orai* time sleep."

I rolled out my bedroll. It had been a long day, what with the golf ladies and the houses. Still, before I went to sleep there was something I needed to ask Aitatxi.

"What's the Mamu?"

"Sure, no, *zuk badakizu Mamu,*" Aitatxi said. "You know Mamu."

"But those kids said the houses were haunted and you said the Mamu was there. Is the Mamu a ghost?"

"Mamu, he no one thing," Aitatxi said.

"Then what is he?"

Aitatxi was quiet for a long moment, and I saw he was looking into the fire as if the answer was written in the flames.

"Mamu, he all things that come before," Aitatxi said. "Some things, they good, some things, they no so good."

"And back at those houses . . ."

"No so good."

The wood crackled as it burned. And like Aitatxi, I stared

into the fire's heart where it burned blue. But the woman's face wasn't there. Instead, I saw Oxea's face dancing in the flames, becoming and unbecoming the Mamu.

"The Mamu scares me." I looked away from the fire.

"Sure, no, Mamu, he no thing be scared of, *gaixua.* Mamu, he like all things in world, some time he good, some time he no so good."

"I think mostly he no so good."

"*Ez,* Mamu, he like rain. On day *eguzkia* burn hot, rain come, it good thing. *Baina,* on cold *gau,* rain come, make *zure* teeth click together, it no so good thing. Mamu, he like rain."

"But how do you know when the Mamu is good or bad?"

"See in face," Aitatxi said.

"I don't want to get that close."

"Only way to know. Mamu, he come you need see in face."

"But how will I know?"

"*Zure behotza*—your heart, it know," Aitatxi said. "*Baina* no more worry, *gaixua.* Tomorrow we climb mountain. Now it time fo—"

"I know, *bu-ba*—bedtime."

"*Ez, bu-ba* for when *mutila*—boy," Aitatxi said. "*Gizona orai*—man now, for you is *lo egitera.*"

"*Lo egitera,*" I said. "Go to sleep."

"*Gauhun,*" Aitatxi said as he lay down. "Good night."

I stretched out on my bedroll and closed my eyes, but I couldn't sleep. I kept thinking about the Mamu and Dad and the sheep and school. Everything was mixed together. I couldn't keep still. My heart was beating fast. I wanted to run—run and run, until I collapsed exhausted on the ground, my head empty of every thought. I'd wished for my life to change quickly, and it had. But now I was sorry for it.

I always thought of change as good. When I didn't like something, change it and it would be better. Only that wasn't how it worked. Change was like the Mamu—sometimes good and sometimes no so good.

Like Oxea dying.

I rolled over onto my back and opened my eyes. I tried to remember which star Aitatxi said was Oxea. But there were so many stars, and only one Oxea. Oxea who talked loud, as if you were across the barn and not standing right in front of him. Oxea who wore his beret pushed back to reveal a forehead creased with dark folds. Oxea who, even though his jacket bulged with the muscles underneath, let me pin him to the barn floor and make him say, "Uncle." I thought Oxea was forever. And maybe he was. Maybe all the stars were Oxea. A little bit of him in each one.

When was his funeral? It seemed like I'd been on the sheep drive for weeks. But when I worked back through time to the morning of my birthday, only three days had passed. Three days. I wished I could go back and live them over. I'd make everything different—talk Dad into letting Aitatxi keep his sheep, make Oxea alive. His funeral was tomorrow.

Would Dad fly back to Denver for it? Maybe that was why he hadn't come for me yet. Maybe he had more important things to do than find me. But no, Dad wasn't like that. He wouldn't leave until he was sure I was safe. Even now he was probably looking up at the same stars I was, thinking about me. He'd be worried. Not sleeping. Like me, he'd have a hundred things banging around in his head. I pictured the gravy stain from a dinner he'd only picked at on his shirt, and him shifting his weight from one foot to the other, thinking about selling the sheep, wishing he hadn't, missing my mom, his dad, me.

And I missed him. The weight of his hand as he ran it through my hair. The deepness of his voice as he told me good night. And even the way he smiled when I caught him staring at me without my knowing. His smile not really a smile, but only the beginning of a smile or maybe the end of one. And I'd tell him to stop it, and he would say, "I love you, son." And I would groan. "God, you're embarrassing me." Right then, lying on the cement floor of Christmas Town, I couldn't remember ever embarrassing him back. I must've. At least once.

My missing Dad was too big to fit inside me. Tears filled my eyes. I wiped them away even as they turned muddy from the dirt covering my skin. Aitatxi began to snore. With each exhale, his breath rattled like a door banging against its frame. One of the sheep stirred in the corner. Its sharp hooves clicked against the cement floor. The sheep began to *baa*. The sound was so sad. It matched how I felt.

After the *baa*ing had gone on for ten minutes, I got up and went over to see if something was wrong. All the sheep were lying down with their heads tucked against their sides except for one—Gaixua. His right front leg was caught in Aitatxi's rope fence.

"What's with all the noise?" I said as I knelt down. "You'd think a coyote had a hold of you."

Gaixua looked at me with watery brown eyes, as if he too had been crying—if sheep could even cry. And instead of hating the helplessness I saw in Gaixua's eyes, I was glad for it. Gaixua needed me, and I could help him. Unlike Oxea or Dad, who were both beyond my reach. My hand closed around the sheep's leg. Wool slid between my fingers as I gripped the leg's bone. I felt the weight of the sheep's body as he leaned against me.

"It's okay, Gaixua. I'm here."

As I untangled his leg, Gaixua put his face right up against mine. His breath was warm against my cheek and smelled like grass rotting in the sun.

"You stink." I pushed him away.

But that didn't stop Gaixua. He nuzzled my neck, and I laughed at the feel of his wet nose against my skin.

"There, you're free," I said as I let go of his leg. "*Zaza lo egitera orai*—go to sleep now."

Gaixua gave a short "*baa*" of agreement and then settled down on the floor and was still. I walked back over to the fire. The flames were gone, and only embers were left. In their faint glow I looked at Atarrabi and Mikelats curled up on either side of Aitatxi. I smiled. The noise in my head had stopped. The night was quiet. It was time for *lo egitera.*

I fell asleep dreaming I was falling up a hole, like Alice in Wonderland. But instead of the Cheshire Cat's grin hanging in the air, it was Gaixua's watery brown eyes that were all around me. And as I fell up, the eyes changed, widening into brown pools. Reflected in those pools was the face of the Mamu, and, while I was no longer afraid, I was still not sure if this Mamu was good or bad.

fifteen | hamaborzt

I woke to voices. They sounded like they were bubbling up from the bottom of a deep well. Streams of unformed words rose, moved together and apart as the voices slowly took shape to break the surface.

I sat up.

The morning light was hazy. Overhead, a ceiling of clouds matched the building's cement walls.

I looked in the direction the voices were coming from and saw Aitatxi talking to a man in a blue uniform. We were caught.

Then Aitatxi turned and saw I was awake.

"*Haugi hunat, gaixua,* meet new friend, Mr. Grants," Aitatxi said.

I got up and cautiously walked over to where they stood.

"You two are quite the story." Mr. Grants held out his hand for me to shake.

"Mr. Grants," Aitatxi said, "he work here. He no is police, *gaixua.*"

I shook his hand.

"My wife is going to flip when I tell her what I found under the Christmas tree." Mr. Grants glanced at his watch.

"What time is it?" I asked.

"Huh," Mr. Grants said, like he hadn't just checked. "Oh, yeah, coming up on seven."

"We should get going, Aitatxi," I said.

"Sure, no," Aitatxi said. "We near trail *orai.* I stay for donuts *baina* us go."

Just then, the three boys from the day before rode their bikes into the building. The freckle-faced boy had a paper sack in his hand. The sides were stained with grease. He came to a skidding stop.

"Donut delivery."

Aitatxi rubbed his hands together and started toward the boys. "*Untxa,* chocolate."

I turned to follow but was stopped by Mr. Grant's hand on my shoulder.

"Can I talk to you a minute, kid," Mr. Grants said, and from the tone of his voice I knew it wasn't a question. He led me a few feet further away from Aitatxi and the boys, then said, "What's your name?"

"Didn't you read it in the paper?"

"I'm not good with names." Mr. Grants smiled. His teeth were straight and white.

"Matt," I said.

"Matt, had an uncle with that name. Look, the thing is . . . how old is your grandpa?"

"Eighty-one. Why?"

"That's not young." Mr. Grants wiped away a line of sweat along his upper lip. "It's going to be a hot one today. Muggy as hell. I even heard there's a chance of an early monsoon."

"I don't mind the heat." I shifted my weight from one leg to the other.

"You, no, but I'd hate to see anything happen to the old guy."

"Nothing's going to happen," I said. Then I added, "Is it?"

Mr. Grants clucked his tongue and cocked his head to the side as he again checked his watch.

"Things happen," Mr. Grants said. "World's a crazy place. People need to be careful. You know what I'm saying, Matt? This whole thing is . . . well . . . over some sheep."

"They're his sheep."

"Not legally," Mr. Grants said. "But maybe he doesn't know that? You do, though, right?"

I watched as Aitatxi ate his donut. There was chocolate smeared on both his cheeks. "*Izigarri gozoak dira*—they very good." He smiled and waved for me to come over. "I eat them all you no come."

"C'mon, kid," Mr. Grants said. "Don't you think it's time you went home?"

And that was what I wanted—to go home. To my room, to my bed. No more sheep, no more desert. Mr. Grants was making it easy for me. It wouldn't even be my fault. What could I do? I was just a kid. Still . . . Aitatxi was teaching the boys to count in Basque. I heard them repeat after him, "*Bagno, bida, hiru, . . .*" I bit the corner of my lip.

"Think of your grandpa," Mr. Grants said.

I squeezed my hands into fists. Dad had told me to look after Aitatxi. Going home was best, for both of us. Gaixua bleated, and I looked over at him and the other sheep in the rope pen. They were all facing me, not making a sound, as if waiting for me to decide.

"After all, they're only sheep, kid," Mr. Grants said.

And he was right. To him they were only sheep. Neither

good nor bad. Nothing to get worked up about. Only sheep. But to Aitatxi—and maybe now a little to me—they were more than that.

"There's a reward," Mr. Grants said, "for the return of the sheep. I'd be willing to give you a little if you help me out."

The morning light was growing brighter, and in that light the sheep's watery eyes glistened like muddy pools. How deep the pools were, I couldn't tell; only the surface was visible to me and reflected there was the face of the Mamu, and it was good.

"What do you say, Matt?"

"*Mendia heltzen da urratz bat aldian,*" I said.

"What's that mean?" Mr. Grants said.

I smiled, "I don't know, but I think I'll stick around and find out. Aitatxi, *joaiten gira.*"

"*Ba.*" Aitatxi started rolling up our bedrolls.

"It's too late." Mr. Grants tapped the face of his watch. "The police will be here any minute."

"*Prishazite orai,*" I said to Aitatxi. "The police are coming."

"Atarrabi, Mikelats, *haugi hunat,*" Aitatxi said. "Mathieu, you get sheeps."

When I started toward the sheep's pen, Mr. Grants tried to grab my arm. "I don't think so, kid."

But I was ready for him. I slid to the side as I ducked and ran forward to pull the pen's top rope—this time on purpose. And just like in the wash, the sheep broke into a mini-stampede, jumping and kicking, their hooves on the cement sounding like a hundred toy popguns going off all at once. The smell of urine and sweat followed the flock as they ran around Mr. Grants.

"Damn it!" He kicked at the sheep, lost his balance and

went down. The flock ran right over him. I saw Snoopy use Mr. Grants's stomach like a trampoline to get a good look around, just to make sure he wasn't missing anything.

As Atarrabi and Mikelats moved the sheep toward the exit, I grabbed my pack and followed the flock and Aitatxi out of the building.

"How far to the secret trail, Aitatxi?" I asked as I caught up to him.

Aitatxi pointed with his walking stick to the foothills. Beyond them, the day's light revealed a mountain.

"Just here," Aitatxi said.

My heart sagged as I saw the hills were several football fields away. Atarrabi and Mikelats would never be able to keep the sheep going fast enough for us to make it. Then I heard whooping behind us and turned around to see the boys popping wheelies on their bikes behind the flock. The sheep broke into a run.

Aitatxi threw back his head and let out an ear-piercing cry. It unwound in the air like a rope thrown toward the top of the mountain. Without thinking, I too let loose my *irrintzina.* Our two cries became one as we ran out across the desert. Or at least I ran. Aitatxi kind of hip-hopped along, using his walking stick like a pole vaulter's pole to make little leaps forward.

By the time we reached the edge of the foothills, I was gulping down air and my sides felt like they were going to split open. Atarrabi and Mikelats, along with the three boys, held the sheep together a little ways ahead. The dogs waited for Aitatxi and directions on which way to go. When Aitatxi got to where I was standing, he leaned forward on his walking stick and waved his beret in front of his face.

"I no more can run like boy," he said.

"Here come the coppers!" the skinny boy yelled.

I looked back to see dust rising behind the two white county sheriff cars driving toward us. Red lights flashed and sirens wailed as the cars bounced over the desert like they were on a roller coaster at Legend City.

"Jail, jail, jail," the littlest boy said.

Straight ahead, there was a group of jagged rocks. Beyond the rocks was the mountain. There was no way the sheriff cars would be able to follow us over the rocks. The deputies would have to come after us on foot, and on foot we might have a chance of losing them. But first we needed to get into the rocks.

"Where's the trail, Aitatxi?"

"*Hemen*—here." Aitatxi pointed at the rocks.

I looked at them for any sign of a trail, but there wasn't any, and the sirens were getting closer.

"There's no trail here, Aitatxi."

"Sure, no, you got . . . how you say . . . get eyes small to see."

"What?"

"Like this." Aitatxi squinted his eyes until they were nearly closed.

"What kind of trail do you have to squint to see?"

"Secret one."

And so I squinted my eyes and looked at the rocks again. And sure enough, through my eyelashes I saw the outline of a trail winding its way up into the mountain.

"What the . . ."

When I opened my eyes wide, the trail disappeared.

"Good trail, *ez?*" Aitatxi said.

"We need to go," I said.

"We'll slow the cops down," the freckle-faced boy said as he turned his bike around and headed straight toward the sheriff cars.

"*Mil esker,*" I shouted as the three boys rode off. "*Izan untxa*—be well."

"Boys good friend," Aitatxi said. "I no think Mr. Grants, he so good friend."

Aitatxi started forward, and I stopped him by grabbing onto his arm.

"I wrote a note on Connie's scorecard telling Dad about the secret trail and the *etxola.*"

"*Zendako?*" Aitatxi said. "Why you do this, *gaixua?*"

"I was scared and homesick an—"

"You no want go a *etxola?*" Aitatxi pushed back his beret and scratched the top of his head.

"Yes, I do want to go . . . now. But before . . . I . . ."

Aitatxi shook his head and didn't say anything. Then he turned away from me, and for the first time since we began the sheep drive, I felt like it would take more than a shower to wash myself clean.

About a hundred yards back, the three boys came to a skidding stop in front of the sheriff cars. They laid down their bikes and slid them under the cars. I cringed when I thought of the scrapes and dents that Pea Picker was going to suffer from the maneuver. The sheriff cars came to a stop, and the two deputies who were driving got out to remove the bikes. When they did, the boys ran in circles around them, screaming and yelling as the deputies tried to grab them.

"Once we get in the rocks, maybe we can go another way," I said.

"*Ez,* only *isileko* trail a *etxola.*" Aitatxi whistled at Atarrabi and Mikelats. "*Ardiak igorri.*" Then with squinted eyes he started up into the foothills as he sang, "*Mendia heltzen da urratz bat aldian.* Take mountain one step at time."

sixteen | hamasei

In a cloud of bleating and dust, the flock struggled to make its way up the rocks. The sheep slipped and bounced against one another. And some of the smaller sheep, like Gaixua, were pushed aside by the bigger ones and tumbled backward. Aitatxi and I caught those sheep and helped them along. When we made it through the rocks, the trail opened up to about four feet and cut to the right.

Aitatxi worked his way to the front of the flock and led the sheep up the slope. I stayed at the back and was glad for the cloud of dust that covered me. I didn't want to be seen by anyone—not the sheep, not Atarrabi and Mikelats, and especially not Aitatxi. Guilt was like rocks in my gut. I'd betrayed Aitatxi. I wanted to apologize for what I did, but I couldn't. That was something my family didn't do. Not because we weren't sorry—I'd have given anything right then not to have written where we were going on that golf card—but because apologies were embarrassing. And not just for the one doing the apologizing, but for the one who had to listen to it as well.

The memory of the last time my dad apologized to me was like a bruise still sore to the touch. It was two months ago, and we were supposed to go to a spring training baseball game. But Dad got home late from work. I was sitting in the dark on the couch when he came in, hating him and wishing he weren't my dad. But as I looked at him framed in the light of the doorway, shoulders slumped and head down like he'd been in a fight and lost, my hate was replaced by fear. I didn't want him like that. I wanted him strong and full of good excuses and to be wrong, wrong, wrong.

Dad didn't see me at first, and when he did he shook his head and instead of saying, "It was work. There was nothing I could do," he said, "I'm sorry, Matt."

The words hit me like cold water. I blinked at the surprise of them. I shifted on the couch, my skin sticking to the upholstery. Why did he have to say that? I wanted to be mad and to sulk and for him to tell me that was just the way things were and for me to tell him, "That sucks" and to be sent to my room and to wake up in the morning with it all over. Like always.

It was just a ball game. Everything didn't have to change over a game. But Dad wouldn't stop. He stood there shifting his weight from one foot to the other, with his head down. I heard him exhale like he'd been holding his breath for a long time and couldn't hold it any longer. Then he said it again—"I'm sorry, Matt." The words rang in my ears as he walked toward me, his shoes squeaking with every step. He ran a hand over the top of his head and sat down beside me on the couch. "Sometimes things happen and you change and you want to change back but you can't."

What was he talking about? My throat was dry and my fingers sweaty where they lay unmoving on the couch. I looked down and began kicking my left heel into the carpet, like I was digging a hole, one I wished I could disappear into. I wouldn't look at him, not like this. I just wanted him to stop.

Dad sighed, and then said, "Okay," real soft like, as if he were saying it to himself and not me. Then he was quiet and we sat there in the dark, neither of us saying anything. He let out another long breath and then his breathing returned to normal. My ears stopped ringing and I quit kicking the floor with my heel. The smell of alfalfa and grease and taco sauce floated around me. I chuckled.

"What's so funny?"

"You had Mexican food for lunch," I said as I gave him a side glance.

"Old Pueblo, the green chile plate," Dad said. "Hungry?"

"Let's get pizza," I said, and with that forgave him.

Dad smiled that not-quite-a-smile of his and said, "I love pizza."

Like Dad, all I could do now was wait for Aitatxi to forgive me with a "See, *gaixua*" or "How you say . . ." And I knew he would—the only question was how long the silence would last.

I checked to see if we were being followed, but the line of rocks we'd come through fell like a curtain between there and here. I listened for a moment and thought I heard the sound of sirens mixing with the whooping of the boys' voices, but then a breeze blew it away. I hustled to catch up with the flock.

When I caught up, Aitatxi said without looking back at me, "You follow I, *gaixua.* I show you how a *mendia heltzen da urratz bat aldian.*"

I smiled and thought, *Mil esker,* Aitatxi.

I turned my attention to the trail we were on. A broken

border of stones marked its edges, only a lot of the stones were missing. In those places, to me anyway, what was and wasn't the trail was hard to tell. But Aitatxi never slowed down; he seemed sure of where he was going.

After we'd walked for about an hour, the creosote became more spread out and the armored trees thinned. Yellow flowers covered the ground. The sheep nibbled at the flowers, which Aitatxi said were "butter weeds" and would keep their bellies full until we reached the *etxola.* Hidden within the butter weeds were baseball-sized cactus that Aitatxi called "sheep-cripplers."

"Also *artzaina*—shepherd-crippler," Aitatxi said. "No step, or big hurt."

Gray trees a little taller than me appeared along the slope. Their trunks were twisted, and Aitatxi said they were pinyon nut pines, but it was too early to eat the nuts. "Oxea and me, we eat nuts in fall when bring sheeps down mountain. Eat *orai,* it break teeth."

And there were other trees, more like scrawny bushes than trees really. Aitatxi said they were oaks.

"*Aritz ona?*" I said.

"*Ez,*" Aitatxi said. "They scrub oak. No is *aritz ona.* When you see *aritz ona,* you know, *gaixua.*"

As we continued to climb, I noticed that the trail wasn't really anything but the easiest way up the mountain where the ground was packed down.

"Who made this trail?"

"We make," Aitatxi said.

"You and Oxea?"

"*Ez,*" Aitatxi said. "We, Eskualdunak—Basques."

Besides my family, I didn't know any other Basques. How many were there? And where did they live? And did they spend their whole lives going up and down this mountain?

"Eskualdunak, we discover this America, *gaixua,*" Aitatxi said.

"That's not what my history book says."

"Book wrong," Aitatxi said. "*Eskualdunak,* we do all kind of great thing, *baina* we no tell no one."

"So pretty much anything one Basque does, we all take credit for?"

"Only good thing. No-good thing, they belong a one alone."

"Does anybody use this trail anymore?"

"Sure, no," Aitatxi said. "We."

Aitatxi whistled and called for the dogs to stop. He took a drink from his *zakua* and I did the same from mine. Then he gazed up at the sun, which, although still covered by clouds, seemed to have turned up its heat. Streaks of sweat ran through the dust and stubble on Aitatxi's cheeks. The smell of sour wine that hung in the air around him was stronger, and his breathing sounded wet and sticky.

"You okay, Aitatxi?"

"High up get at me," Aitatxi said. "Oxea, he got no problem. Oxea, he say air better up here, can get bigger breaths."

The sheep bleated louder than usual.

"I listen you, *ardiak,*" Aitatxi said. "*Ura* near."

"Isn't it time for lunch?"

"We get a *ura* first."

"How much farther?"

"*Baina* here." Aitatxi pointed with his walking stick to a ridge of rocks ahead. "Over rock. It where Oxea find *iturritza.* We take good break from *eguzkia* then."

I licked my dry lips as we started up toward the rocks. I felt a rush of energy at just the thought of water. I broke into a jog. The sheep followed me. Their heads were all up, and their noses in the air, as if they could smell the water ahead.

But before we reached the ridge, Aitatxi yelled, "*Geldi!*"

As I came to a quick stop, several sheep bumped into my legs and I spread my feet to keep from falling over.

"What's wrong?"

"*Isilik,*" Aitatxi said. "Listen."

At first I didn't hear anything but the *baaa*ing of the sheep. But then, from far away, there was a buzzing, like a saw cutting down a tree deep in the forest. A dark spot appeared within the clouds. It moved toward us from the direction we'd come.

"They're looking for us," I said.

"No move."

"Shouldn't we try and hide?"

"We hide by no moving," Aitatxi said.

I held my breath as the plane got nearer. I watched as it passed to the right of us and for a moment was blocked from sight by the ridge. When the plane became visible again, it was heading away.

Was Dad on that plane? Searching the ground for me and Aitatxi? Without thinking I started to raise my hand into the air, wanting to wave and yell, "We're here." But then I stopped. I had betrayed Aitatxi once, I wasn't going to do it again. For bad or good, I was in this sheep drive until the end. I felt like I had when I started my second fire. It was in the oleanders behind school, and the wind came up and the flames jumped to over ten feet high. Before I realized what was happening, the fire was out of control. I tried to put it out. I kicked at the flames and threw handfuls of dirt onto them, but nothing worked. I couldn't stop it. The fire burned the whole row of oleanders, and I ended up at the police station, stinking of smoke and waiting for Dad to come. It was like I'd started another fire now, and there was no way I was going to be able to put it out without getting caught.

When the plane didn't circle back, Aitatxi said, "*Joaiten gira.* We go *ura* now."

But when we cleared the ridge where Oxea's spring was supposed to be, there was nothing but more rocks. Aitatxi took off his beret and scratched his head.

"I guess it went dry," I said.

Thunder rumbled overhead, but the clouds were thin and looked as empty as my *zakua* felt.

"Maybe there's another hidden spring?"

"*Ez,*" Aitatxi said, "this only one."

Aitatxi looked at the dry spring, and I could see his jaw clenching and unclenching.

"How far is it to next *ura?*" I said.

"No *ura* before *etxola.*" Aitatxi shifted his weight from one foot to the other.

"Can the sheep make it?"

"This no is right." Aitatxi gripped his walking stick with both hands. His knuckles turned white with anger. "*Aita, zendako nahi duzu hori egin eni?* Father, why you do this a me?" He raised his walking stick into the air and shook it at the sky. Then he hit the rocks. "*Ura orai!* Water now!" When nothing happened, Aitatxi did it again—"*Ura orai!*" The stick cracked in his hands, and he threw it at the rocks, where it broke into two pieces. Aitatxi fell to his knees.

I held my breath. Something was really wrong. It wasn't Aitatxi's getting mad that scared me. I'd seen him mad before. It was what he got mad about—water.

Aitatxi was breathing hard when he got to his feet. He leaned on a boulder for support. Then he took off his beret and ran a hand through his white hair as he mumbled to himself.

"Are you okay, Aitatxi?"

"We go now, Ferdinand," Aitatxi said, and without looking at me took a shaky step back onto the trail. I reached out to steady him and Aitatxi grabbed onto my arm. His grip was like stone. I knew that grip—I was three and fell into the neighbor's pool. I wasn't supposed to go near the water, but I did. I was alone. The water held me down. I couldn't scream. The world was silent. My lungs were on fire. And then Dad was there. He pulled me out and I grabbed onto his shirt with fingers that had turned to stone.

"It's going to be all right," I said to Aitatxi. The same words Dad had said to me that day. And Aitatxi turned to me with the same glazed eyes I had looked at my father with, eyes gone wide with the whiteness of death.

seventeen | hamazazpi

Aitatxi held on to me as we walked in silence. I kept telling myself that every step was bringing me closer to Dad. He would be coming down the trail from the *etxola;* any moment he'd appear, angry and relieved. But where was he? Miles away or only steps? It was his fault I was here. He shouldn't have left me behind. My fear turned to anger of my own. Right then I hated my father for doing this to me and to Aitatxi—his own dad. This was all my dad's fault. Didn't he know Aitatxi at all? If Dad did, he wouldn't have sold the sheep. But maybe Dad couldn't see it? Like with me and my fires. After the oleander fire, the policeman told Dad that next time I started a fire, I'd be arrested and prosecuted. Dad told him there wouldn't be a next time.

When we got home from the police station, Dad followed me into my room. There, I flopped onto my bed and stared at the ceiling as he paced back and forth.

"Why in hell would you start those oleanders on fire?" Dad said.

"I don't know," I said, but I did know and I wanted to tell

Dad. But the words got all bunched together in my throat.

"That's not good enough," Dad said. "What were you thinking?"

"I . . . I had to," I said, and with those words I wanted him to understand it all, how I needed him to stay, here, with me, always. How I wanted to wake up every morning and hear him moving around in the kitchen and go to bed seeing his shirt stained with that night's dinner.

"No, you didn't." Dad stood at the foot of my bed and looked down at me. "I'm really disappointed in you, Matt. I mean, someone could have gotten hurt. Now maybe you don't care about that, but I'd—"

"I care," I said.

"They why would you choose to start a fire?"

Why couldn't he see? I wasn't choosing anything. He forced me to light the fire. My breaths came short and fast, my lips forming all the things I wanted to explain to Dad, only I didn't know how to start and where to end. All the things I needed to say to him had gotten too big for the words I knew.

"Now, then," Dad said, "no more fires. Understood?"

And I lied and said I did.

Little by little, Aitatxi's grip on my arm loosened, and after an hour or so he was walking on his own again.

I searched the sky for signs of the plane. The way we'd come couldn't be hard to find. The police wouldn't even need tracking dogs to follow the scent of thirty-two stinking sheep. So where were they? The trail we were on began to fade. The rocks marking it disappeared, and Aitatxi stopped every few feet to look at the ground before going on. He kept calling me Ferdinand and speaking to me in Basque. But he used words I didn't understand.

We kept going.

After a while, larger trees replaced the pinyon pines. The new trees' bark was thick and cracked. I didn't have the energy to ask Aitatxi the name of the trees. By then, I was having trouble swallowing. It smelled like rain, but none fell. We walked beneath a group of tall pines; under their limbs the air thickened. I couldn't catch my breath. My shirt stuck to my body with sweat. The water from my *zakua* was gone.

"*Prishazizte,*" Aitatxi said as the flock's pace began to slow. But Atarrabi and Mikelats didn't even raise their ears at the command. A little after that, Gaixua lay down and wouldn't get up. When I tried to lift him to his feet, I stumbled under his weight.

"Come on," I said. "*Guazen.*"

But Gaixua just stayed where he lay, his head on the ground, his pink tongue hanging from his mouth.

"We come back for," Aitatxi said. "Go now, Ferdinand."

"I'm Matt—Matt, not Ferdinand. Can't you see that?"

"Sure, no," Aitatxi said and turned to look at me.

"Why don't we stay here, Aitatxi? Stay and wait for Dad to come?"

"He no coming," Aitatxi said.

"Sure he will. Remember, I told him about the *etxola* and the secret trail."

Aitatxi took off his beret and, like he had two days earlier in my class, began working the edge through his fingers.

"I sorry, *gaixua,*" Aitatxi said.

"Don't say that."

"I trick you, me both this time."

"No, no, Dad's coming," I said.

"This no is *etxola* Oxea and me, we go each year."

"But you said there was only one secret trail?"

"Sure, no, all *etxola* got own *isileko* trail. *Zure aita,* he thinking we go other *etxola*, one Oxea and me, we go on. *Baina* he go look at other secret trail."

"Dad's not coming to save me?"

"No, *gaixua*, no save," Aitatxi said and put his beret back on his head. "*Joaiten gira.*"

"I'm sorry," I said as I ran my hand over Gaixua's head. The sheep looked at me for a moment, then closed his eyes. I blinked back tears and got to my feet. I followed after Aitatxi.

The trees grew closer together, and as the sheep moved through them they spread out. Atarrabi and Mikelats gave up trying to keep the flock together. The dogs walked beside Aitatxi, their tongues hanging out, their sides caving in with each breath. One by one the sheep wandered off through the trees. I saw Rollo go—he was number six. And then Snoopy turned around and headed back the way we'd come. I called after him, but he kept going, *baa*ing as if calling to his mother. Aitatxi mumbled something about "*Ardiak* all lost," but he didn't stop walking.

Thunder rumbled through the clouds as if trying to shake water from them. But no rain came loose. I turned to follow Aitatxi and tripped over the root of a pine. I fell. Dust filled my mouth, and I didn't have any spit to get it out.

"Aitatxi, wait," I called to his dark back.

But Aitatxi kept walking. He said something about the Pyrenees and raised a hand into the air as if he were talking to someone beside him.

"Aitatxi!"

But he didn't seem to hear me. Mikelats came up beside me and licked my face. I pushed the dog away as I watched Atarrabi follow after Aitatxi. The two of them disappeared into the trees.

I was going to die.

It wasn't so much a surprise as a fact. Just like it wasn't surprising that Oxea killed himself. It was a fact. Or that I would never see Dad again. It was a fact. Like something written in my history book at school. A fact that was and couldn't be changed. And now my death would be a fact too. The thought of death didn't scare me like it did late at night when I was alone in my bedroom. Then death frightened me with all the things it would take away: my dad, Aitatxi, baseball. But now, death made me feel better by what it might give me—my mother.

"Mom," I said. Then I said her name twice more and closed my eyes and settled my head down on the pine needles.

I seemed to be floating. Everything was gray and getting grayer. I don't know how long I floated in that gray world before the light appeared. It was orange and came through my closed eyelids. The light changed to yellow. Then white. I opened my eyes.

The sun had broken through the clouds. Sunshine fell through the limbs of the pine above me so that strings of light filled the tree. I got to my knees. Then, even as the light grew brighter, its center darkened, and the woman of my fires took shape. She wore a dress of flames and was surrounded by gold. I blinked, but she didn't go away. It was Mari, the queen of the genies.

Mari's face was covered by a shadow as she reached toward me with her right hand. At first I thought she wanted me to take her hand so that she could fly me up to heaven. But then I saw how her palm was open like she was waiting for me to place something in it. I remembered what Aitatxi said about Mari needing a gift. But what? A sheep? Even if I wanted to, right then I didn't have the strength to pick up a sheep. I needed to give her something else. Something from my *bihotza*. I took Oxea's beret from my head.

I held the beret up toward Mari. The light around her dimmed, and for a moment, I saw the profile of her face and the familiar line of her jaw. She turned to gaze down at me and smiled, her green eyes lit with flames. And in those eyes I recognized my mother.

A gust of wind that went from hot to cold even as it blew over me lifted Oxea's beret out of my hand. The black hat flew into the air, up through the limbs of the pine. Higher and higher Oxea's beret went, above the green treetops, and still it rose, until it became a solitary black dot in the sky. Then, as Oxea's beret disappeared into the clouds, it started to rain. The clouds again closed over the sun, and when I looked back at where Mari had been, she was gone.

Water dripped from the branches of the pine and fell onto my face. I closed my eyes and saw my mother the way she was in the picture I stole from Dad's dresser. The picture I'd slipped unseen into my desk at school, not wanting to have to explain to Rich and the other kids that the woman was my mother, only I needed a picture to remember what she looked like. But the picture I saw now was different, like it was taken right before the other one. In it, my mother still leans out the pickup's window waving, but whatever it is that will take away her smile is still in the future. In this moment her green eyes flash. Her cheeks are red with laughter, and her chin goes to a point—just like mine.

eighteen | hamazortzi

My relief at the falling rain didn't last long. The sprinkles hitting my face grew harder. Lightning cracked in the sky. Then it was like someone flicked a switch and the lights went out. The day became a starless night. Mikelats whined. And as I reached toward him, a bomb seemed to explode right above me. Mikelats was thrown into the air; he yelped as he hit the ground. I was pushed flat onto the dirt by what felt like a giant hand. All the wind was knocked out of me and it took a moment for me to get a good breath.

From where I lay, I saw the last of the sheep scatter. They ran blindly through the wall of rain. Some of them collided with the trunks of trees, others trampled me, their sharp hooves hitting my head like rocks. The whole world seemed to be coming together and flying apart at the same time.

First no rain and now this. It wasn't fair. None of it. I hadn't wanted to go on the sheep drive. I was forced. Had no choice. Nobody asked me. Not my dad who was always gone and not Oxea who hung himself over some stupid sheep. Or Aitatxi who . . . Aitatxi? Where was Aitatxi? Was he hurt? Did he need me?

"Aitatxi," I yelled, but got no answer. I scrambled to my feet. The wind let up a little, but the pouring rain continued to fall. Some of the day's light was returning, and I could see a few feet in front of me. Mikelats sat at the base of a tree as if waiting for me.

"Mikelats, Aitatxi *joan!* Go to Aitaxti!"

Mikelats turned and ran in the direction Aitatxi had gone. I stumbled after the barking dog. Twice I slipped and fell into the mud. Another time I ran into a low-hanging tree limb. The blow to my head made my eyes water, but I didn't stop. I had to find Aitatxi. Lightning cut across the sky. And in its light I saw a black circle on the ground. I ran forward and picked up Aitatxi's beret.

"Aitatxi!"

Up ahead, Mikelats's barking was joined by Atarrabi's. I rushed forward, pushing aside tree branches, and stepped into a clearing. The two dogs stood on either side of Aitatxi, who lay facedown on the trail.

"Aitatxi?"

I knelt beside my grandfather and pulled off his pack. I rolled him over. Mud covered his face, and pine needles were stuck in his hair. The cut on his forehead was bleeding again, and the blood ran down into his eyes. I used the handkerchief from around Aitatxi's neck to wipe it away.

"Aitatxi?"

He didn't move. I started to cry.

"Aitatxi, please don't go."

Then, without opening his eyes, Aitatxi said, "Sure, no, I no dead yet, *gaixua.* Only resting." He looked up at me with a tiny smile.

Aitatxi's not being dead made me cry even harder. I put my head on his chest and hugged him.

"I love you, Aitatxi."

"I know this, *gaixua.*"

By the time I lifted my head off of Aitatxi, the falling rain had washed away all the day's heat. Cold took its place. Aitatxi shivered. I needed to get him out of the rain. I helped him to his feet, and in silence we started forward as Atarrabi and Mikelats slipped back to gather the remaining sheep.

As we went, Aitatxi kept his hand on my shoulder, leaning on me like I was his walking stick. I was searching for someplace to get dry when I spotted the cave.

"Oxea, his cave," Aitatxi said. "No like *iturritza,* it still here."

I walked Aitatxi into the cave and sat him down. There was a stack of firewood along one of the walls, and I started to gather the wood to make a fire.

"I do," Aitatxi said. "You pen sheeps."

I pulled off my pack and took out the rope. I was about to ask Aitatxi if there was any more rope in his pack when I realized we'd left his pack back on the trail. Tomorrow I'd go and get it. But for now I'd have to make do with the rope I had. It was time to take care of the sheep.

I stepped out into the rain. It was letting up a little, but the clouds were still dark. I couldn't tell what time it was, but it had to be getting late, close to dusk. With Atarrabi and Mikelats's help, I got the sheep inside. The smell of wet wool they brought with them filled the cave and made my eyes burn. I breathed through my mouth as I blinked away tears.

I got the sheep to the back of the cave, and there, Atarrabi and Mikelats held them in place while I looked for something to tie the rope to. What I found were pegs of wood jammed into cracks in the rock. The pegs were perfectly spaced to make a rope pen. After I made sure my knots would hold, I counted what was left of the flock—fourteen was all. Rollo made it, Snoopy didn't.

I planned to go back for Aitatxi's pack in the morning. I might be able to find a few more sheep—including Gaixua, if he was still alive. I was about to tell Aitatxi this when I saw that he'd fallen asleep while building the fire. His head was leaning forward on his chest. The wood was scattered in front of him, one piece still in his hand.

As I walked back over to Aitatxi, a breeze blew through the cave, and for a moment it took away the smell of sheep and replaced it with pine and rain. My head cleared and I again heard Aitatxi's words—*mendia heltzen da urratz bat aldian.* That was what I would do now—take the mountain one step at a time. That was how I would make it to the *etxola.*

I went to my pack and took out my bedroll. It was in the middle of my extra clothes and pretty much dry. I spread the bedroll out on the cave's floor and, after taking off Aitatxi's wet coat, pants, and shoes, I helped him onto it. He said something about *ardien begiak,* then started to snore. Atarrabi went over and stretched out beside Aitatxi as Mikelats came to curl up at my feet.

After getting the wood together, I spent about ten minutes trying to light one of the damp matches from my pack. At first none of the matches would even spark. Still, I wasn't too worried—starting fires was one thing I was good at. When I finally got the fire going, I took out what was left of my bread. I put some aside for Aitatxi and then split up the rest between me and the dogs. Mikelats gulped his down, but Atarrabi wouldn't even sniff the bread I left sitting beside him on the bedroll.

While I ate the stale bread, I threw more wood on the fire. It crackled as it grew. In the fire's light, I looked down at my hands. There was dirt under my fingernails and the knuckle of my right thumb was scabbed over with dried blood. I turned my hands over. The skin of my palms was scratched, and in the flickering light, I couldn't tell which lines I'd always had and which were new.

Even though Aitatxi was only ten feet away, I felt alone. I wasn't afraid. Just a little sad. And I wasn't exactly sure why. It was like I'd crossed a bridge that went from one side of a canyon to the other, and now that bridge was gone and I couldn't go back the way I'd come. I thought about checking under my arms for hair, but didn't. My *zakua* was empty, so I picked up Aitatxi's. The bitter red wine made my throat catch, but I swallowed it anyway.

nineteen | hamaretzi

The cave became warmer as the fire's flames reached higher. Light bounced off the walls, and in the light, I saw black marks on the rock of the cave's back wall. I was too busy penning the sheep and taking care of Aitatxi to notice them earlier. Now I went over to check them out. The smell of smoke from past fires was on the wall, and up close I saw that the black marks had been made with charcoal and formed a picture.

In the middle of the picture there were swirling circles like miniature clouds with legs that I realized were sheep. On either side of the sheep was a dog with a long tail, slinking forward. Behind the sheep walked two men: a larger man with a round head to match his round belly and a skinny man with an impossibly hooked nose. Each man wore a flat hat on his head and carried a walking stick in his hand.

"Oxea and Aitatxi," I laughed.

Then I saw the boy. He was walking a little way behind the two men. And even though it was a charcoal drawing with smeared edges, there was something familiar in the way the boy stepped forward, something I knew in the way he held his arms.

"Dad," I said.

The fire popped behind me as the shadow of my hand moved over the drawing to touch the sheep, the dogs, the men, and finally, came to rest on the boy. Behind the boy was a trail marked with a broken line. There was an *X* on some rocks with wiggly lines like running water around them. The word "*iturritza*" was written there. I looked to the front of the sheep and saw the same broken line winding its way up a mountain. Along the way were other *X*'s marked with "*zaza eskain*" and "*zaza zuzen.*" And there was a dark circle like the opening of the cave I stood in. It was marked with "*oxean shokua*" and after that was written "*egun bat gehiago.*"

"*Egun bat gehiago.* One more day," I said as I followed the broken line to a large tree, the kind of tree a kid would draw, with a straight trunk and a round top. Written beneath the tree was "*Harrapatu aritz ona.*"

"Look for the good oak," I said and saw that next to the tree the trail ended with the word "*etxola.*" I stepped away from the wall and looked at the whole map drawn there.

"*Zure aita,* he draw when he you age," Aitatxi said, and I turned to see him sitting up. "He think maybe Oxea and me, we get lost on next sheeps drive."

"So then Dad knows about this secret trail?"

"He only go on this trail one time," Aitatxi said. "I no think he remember. After then, only Oxea and me go. Before now."

"Dad never told me he went on any sheep drive."

I grabbed Aitatxi's *zakua* and handed it to him. He took a long drink.

"Sure, no," Aitatxi said, with red wine dripping down his chin. "First time, right after Oxea's wife, Pascaline, she die. Ferdinand, he love Pascaline very much. So he no want a go funeral."

"Because he loved her?"

"*Beti besala*—like always, that way with Ferdinand." Aitatxi set the *zakua* down. "Things he no like, *ene semea* move away from, he think then maybe no hurt so much. I tell him it no work like that. *Baina* Ferdinand, he no listen. Pascaline die, Ferdinand, he run away from home. I find him three mile down road. He in big-time trouble. I make go on sheeps drive. He so mad, he no smile at all. *Baina*, further we get from home, the more Ferdinand, he like. Every step he take, Ferdinand, he no scowl so much. He no want a go home when over." Aitatxi sighed. "My Ferdinand, he love sheeps before . . ."

"Before what?"

"Ferdinand, he forgot."

"Forgot what?"

"Past, *gaixua*," Aitatxi said.

"Why'd he forget?"

"When *zure ama*, she die, *zure aita*, he no want a think about past—about sheeps drive, or Basque way. All things before then, they make him sad for *zure ama*. Ferdinand, he put them all away. He think past all no good. Ferdinand, he no remember good past. You make him remember, *gaixua*."

"Me?"

"*Ba*, say about pretty lady in golf cart, and about Mamu houses, and good boys. Say about storm and cave."

"How's that going to help?"

"That you past now," Aitatxi said. "After then, you ask Aita say about his past."

"Why don't you ask him?"

Aitatxi didn't answer me. He just said again, "Make him remember, *gaixua.* You only one now." Then he took another drink of wine.

I sat down on a rock next to the fire and waited until Aitatxi stopped shooting the thin thread of wine from the *zakua* into his mouth, then I said, "What are we going to do once we get to the *etxola?*"

"Go home," Aitatxi said.

"That's it? We've done all this just to go home?"

"How you want a do?"

"I don't know, something—a party maybe."

"Sure, no, they no party for sheeps drive."

"Well, there should be," I said. "Next time w—"

"They no next time, *gaixua,*" Aitatxi said. "This last sheeps drive."

"Why do you say that?"

"Things they change very much," Aitatxi said. "Sheeps drive good thing, but it past. Good for remember." Aitatxi stared off into the night. "Maybe you come on trail again, only no *ardiak.* Maybe come with *zure aita.*"

All the talk of Dad brought the dryness from earlier in the day back to my mouth.

"After this, I don't think Dad will be letting me go anywhere for a while."

"I no so sure," Aitatxi said. "Only tell him how he like when young."

"But I don't know what he was like when he was my age," I said. "He never talks about it."

"Oh, *ene* Ferdinand, he wild thing," Aitatxi said. "He wear Amatxi out."

"Dad?"

"Sure, no, you no want to know thing he done."

"Yeah, I do." I leaned toward Aitatxi. "Give."

"Once time, Oxea, he make *sagar arnoa*—apple wine. Only he no know how a make. But my Ferdinand, he sneak in and drink Oxea's no-so-good wine."

"What happened?"

"He get sick all in garden, kill Amatxi's vegetables."

I laughed. "I can't wait to ask him about it."

"You no get wrong, *gaixua.* My Ferdinand, he good boy."

"But wild," I said.

"*Puxkat,*" Aitatxi said as he scratched Atarrabi's head. "He all time playing *pelote.*"

"Dad played *pelote?*"

"Sure, no, Ferdinand, he love handball, he bang ball against side of barn until Amatxi, she say it making her crazy."

"Dad sure got into a lot of trouble."

"*Puxkat,*" Aitatxi said. "I wish I take him a Pyrenees more."

"What's so great about the Pyrenees?"

"Pyrenees, they most beautiful place on earth. That because they no earth, *baina* heaven. So green hurt *zure begiak* a see."

"Maybe I'll go someday."

"Sure, no, you go," Aitatxi said. "See there me. I be with Amatxi and Oxea and *zure ama.* We all waiting for you come."

I didn't point out that two days before, Aitatxi had said Amatxi, Oxea, and my mom were stars in the sky. I'd learned that in Aitatxi's world anything was possible. Besides, I liked the idea of Oxea being with Amatxi and Mom in heaven. But I wondered if it was possible after what Oxea had done.

"You think God will let Oxea in heaven, after . . . you know . . ."

Aitatxi nodded his head slowly. "Always know, *gaixua*, God, he got much bigger *bihotza* than man."

"Is that so God can love man more?"

"*Ez,* it so God, he can forgive man more," Aitatxi said.

I threw another stick on the fire and said, "Tell me about my mother."

"Sure, no, that little *neska,* she get into everything." Aitatxi took another drink of wine from his *zakua.*

"Excellent." I settled in to listen.

That night Aitatxi told me about how my mother only rode horses bareback, and how my father broke his arm jumping out of the hayloft, and how Oxea forgot how to say "I do" in English on his wedding day. Each story Aitatxi told me he had a little less English in it until, as it got later, he slipped into pure Basque. I didn't mind. I could tell when he talked slow that he was saying something serious, and I knew by his raised eyebrows when to laugh. And somewhere during the telling, I made a point to remember everything he said, even the words whose meaning I'd yet to learn.

The last thing Aitatxi said before he fell asleep was in English. "I no forget you birthday, *gaixua.* I know just what I going a give you."

"I don't want anything, Aitatxi," I replied, and at that moment I meant it.

twenty | hogei

Right before I woke that morning, I dreamed of a place so green it hurt my eyes. Clouds covered the tops of mountains that seemed to be cut from emeralds. A river tumbled down between the mountains, the water becoming a hundred whispering voices as it flowed out into a meadow. Sun-yellow flowers lined a path that wound its way through the meadow and into the distance. I wanted to follow that path, to go where it led, to get lost in those green mountains. But I couldn't. Not yet. Heaven still scared me.

The world I belonged to was one of rock and sheep and a father who, for the first time in my life, I realized might need me more than I did him. So I opened my eyes and shivered in the cold of the cave.

I expected to find Aitatxi up already, outside searching for stray sheep or having himself a "firm pee," but he was still lying on his bedroll. I figured he was worn out from the day before. I'd let him sleep. I decided to start a fire to warm up the cave for when he woke up. I heard Atarrabi whine. He was sitting beside Aitatxi. Mikelats was standing at the edge of the cave where shadow turned to light.

"Atarrabi, Mikelats, *haugi hunat,*" I said in a hushed voice, so as not to wake Aitatxi. But neither dog came. "*Haugi,*" I said again, but the dogs stayed where they were, their eyes fixed on Aitatxi. I held my breath and listened for Aitatxi's raspy breathing, but the only sound came from the wind blowing through the pines outside.

"Aitatxi?" I said and on hands and knees I crawled over to him. "Aitatxi?"

The cave seemed to grow colder as I rested my head on Aitatxi's chest. His *bihotza* was silent. The world slowed. Stopped.

"Aitatxi." I grabbed onto his shoulders and shook him. "Wake up, wake up."

But he didn't.

My breaths came short and sharp. What was happening? All the air in the cave seemed to have disappeared. Aitatxi? He was just resting, that was all. He would open his eyes in a moment and say, "*Ttipia eta itsusia. Bildotsa gaixua.*" Any moment now.

I squeezed my eyes closed against the tears I couldn't keep from coming. And when I did, I saw Aitatxi. He was walking up a path lined with sun-yellow flowers toward Oxea and Amatxi and Mom.

"No—Aitatxi, come back!"

But it was too late. Aitatxi was gone. And I was left with another hole in me that I didn't know how I'd ever fill.

I felt light-headed. There was nothing left to anchor me to this world. My body seemed to be rising off the cave's rock floor, up toward a mountain of green. Then I heard the sheep. Their *baa*ing echoed off the cave walls. They'd be thirsty, need water. There might be some pools left over from the rain, and I still might be able to find a few more of the flock lost in the trees. Like stones the thoughts weighed me down. The rocks of the cave's floor cut into my knees. My Aitatxi was dead, who cared about some stinking sheep? But the sheep were mine now. A last trick played on me by Aitatxi. My birthday present.

I don't know how long I stayed there on the stone floor. I cried some, but then I stopped. Mikelats put his head on my lap. The sheep bleated. It was time to get going.

I got to my feet and went to the map on the wall. I figured I could use it to find the *aritz ona* and the *etxola.* Still, I was alone on top of a mountain, with fourteen sheep. How was I going to make it? *Mendia heltzen da urratz bat aldian.* Take the mountain one step at a time.

I went back to Aitatxi and took hold of the edge of the bedroll. Atarrabi and Mikelats followed me as I dragged the bedroll to the back of the cave. There, I knelt down and ran a finger over the stubble of Aitatxi's cheek. The cut on his forehead had never had time to heal. Dried blood was caked around its edges. I spit on my fingers and cleaned the blood away. Then I smoothed back Aitatxi's hair and folded his hands on his chest before gently wrapping him in the bedroll.

I left the dogs to watch over Aitatxi's body as I walked out of the cave.

Outside, the sun was warm on my face. Singing birds filled the air. I breathed in the scent of pines. It seemed impossible that anything could die on a day like this. Then I looked back down the trail we came on and saw the body of Snoopy lying there. The sheep's throat was ripped open; his guts spilled over the dirt. The bloody pawprints of coyotes were on the ground. I wouldn't be finding any lost sheep. At least none that were alive.

While I felt bad for Snoopy, I felt worse for myself. If I didn't make it to the *etxola* by nightfall, I'd be out in the open with only the dogs to help me protect the sheep from the coyotes, who'd had a taste of blood and would want more. I needed to hurry. My only chance was to find the *aritz ona* before it got dark. But I couldn't just leave Aitatxi's body to the coyotes. The idea of Aitatxi and the body that was in the cave were different things to me. What lay in the cave was no longer my Aitatxi but a suit he had worn and left behind. He wore a new suit now as he hiked up a mountain of green. Still, the thought of leaving his body to be picked over by coyotes made my jaw clench with anger. So I started gathering rocks to cover Aitatxi's body. I don't know how long it took for me to complete the grave. After about twenty rocks, it felt like one of them was stuck between my shoulder blades. My body seemed to move on its own. I started to sing. It was a crazy song to Bread's "Everything I Own." The lyrics came out half in English and half in Basque.

When the grave was done, I knew I needed to say something, but I didn't know the right words—in English or Basque. I should have asked Aitatxi how you say good-bye, if not forever, for a long time. And now it was too late. All I could think about were the other things I'd forgotten to ask him:

How long did it take for Aitatxi to finally ask Amatxi to marry him?

What did Amatxi say? Sure, yes?

When did they leave the Basqueland?

Why did they come to Arizona?

Were they afraid?

Did Oxea and his wife come with them?

What color were Pascaline's eyes?

Was the Mamu on the boat that brought them over?

When he was my age, did my dad ever sing songs like Aitatxi?

Did my mother sing along with him?

Did they sing to me?

Questions filled my head. Questions I could have asked Aitatxi while we fed the chickens or ate a meal of cheese and bread or as he turned off the lights with the words "*Gauhun, gaixua,*" but I hadn't. I bit my lip at all the missed chances. At least there was still my dad. He could answer some if not all of my questions.

"*Nik aitai eginaraziko dut oraitzea,*" the words coming to me. "I promise I'll make my dad remember." Then I put on Aitatxi's beret, "*Mil esker,* Aitatxi, for taking me on this sheeps drive. *Izan untxa*—be well."

I needed to get going, not to think too much, just take that first step up the mountain. I went to the sheep pen and called to the dogs, "*Joaiten gira.*"

But Atarrabi and Mikelats just looked at me from beside Aitatxi's grave.

"*Haugi hunat,* Atarrabi, Mikelats." I gave a short whistle.

The sheep's hooves clattered on the cave floor—it was time to go. But I couldn't go anywhere without the dogs. I walked over to them and knelt down.

"Look, I'm sorry I said you were lazy and stupid. I didn't know. But you can't stay here. I need you. Please."

The dogs didn't seem to hear me as they closed their eyes and put their heads down on the cave floor. The reality of getting the sheep up to the *etxola* set in. Even with Aitatxi, Atarrabi, and Mikelats, we lost over half the sheep. Now, alone, without any help, I couldn't make it.

But what if I left the sheep behind with the dogs? I'd be able to move faster alone, probably make it to the *etxola* in a few hours. Maybe by then Dad would remember about the secret trail he took when he was my age. Even now, he might be waiting for me beneath the *aritz ona.* Dad wouldn't blame me for leaving the sheep. No one would. And besides, I could always come back and get the sheep with Dad . . . that is, if they were still alive.

What if Atarrabi and Mikelats couldn't fight off the coyotes? Right then, I wasn't even sure the dogs would try. And then there was Aitatxi; he'd want me to finish the "sheeps drive."

I sat down on the cave floor. I couldn't do it. I was sorry, but it was too much. There was heat behind my eyes. I tried not to cry, but tears slid down my cheeks. I just wanted to go home. Then I felt Mikelats's warm tongue on my face as he licked my tears away.

"Stupid dog." I pushed Mikelats away. He barked as he danced around me. But not Atarrabi; he remained where he lay. "Atarrabi?"

Mikelats nuzzled Atarrabi, and I tried to lift him to his feet. But it was no use, Atarrabi collapsed back onto the floor. He wasn't going anywhere. I understood. Atarrabi wanted to stay with Aitatxi. So had I. Now at least one of us would. I stroked Atarrabi's head and said, "I'll come back for you." Then I went over to study the map one last time.

The map showed how the trail rose steadily after leaving the cave. There also seemed to be some kind of steep climb right before reaching the *etxola*, but it didn't look too bad. If I kept the sheep close to the side of the mountain, I'd be all right until I spotted the oak marking the *etxola.* I hoped Dad was right when he wrote that it was only one more day to the *etxola.*

I put Atarrabi's bread from the night before beside him, patted his head, and again promised to come back for him. I put the bread Aitatxi hadn't eaten into my pack for me and Mikelats. Then with Mikelats's help, I moved the sheep out of the cave.

Outside, I found a muddy pool for the flock to drink from. And as the sheep and Mikelats drank, I filled my *zakua* from a low spot where water gathered in the rocks. When I lowered my mouth to suck up the last of the water, the sun was hot on the back of my neck. I looked up to see sunlight flickering through the trees. It was already past noon. My eyes moved over to Snoopy's body on the trail.

"*Guazen*, Mikelats," I said.

Mikelats let out a series of barks that sent the sheep forward. I took a last look at the cave. For a moment sunlight filled it, and I saw the drawing on the back wall, and Aitatxi's grave with Atarrabi beside it. Then the shadow of the mountain fell over the opening, and the cave grew dark. It appeared a lot deeper than I knew it was. Right then, the cave seemed to tunnel back into the mountain, and I imagined it winding its way into the rock, one cave connecting to another, and Mari flying through them all in a flame of light.

I turned away and followed the sheep up the mountain.

twenty-one | hogeibat

Like the map showed, the trail went up after we left the cave. The slope wasn't much, and the sheep moved along quickly. Mikelats didn't have any trouble keeping the flock together. After everything that had happened the day before, I didn't think any of the sheep were too eager to wander off.

The pines grew thicker and the other trees slipped away. Soon the trail was again clearly marked with rocks. I wondered if Dad had put them there? With Aitatxi telling his Ferdinand to "mark good" so that next time they could clearly see the way. But there was no next time on this trail for my dad. Why? Why didn't he come on this secret trail for another sheep drive? Then I thought about what Aitatxi said, about how Dad was forced to come because he ran away from Pascaline's funeral. But Aitatxi said Dad was happy to get away from home. "Every step he take, Ferdinand, he no scowl so much." But why? Was it because he was leaving Pascaline's death behind? Was that it? It was hard to know. Dad at my age wasn't easy for me to imagine.

But then I thought about how Dad was now. Was he really so different from back then? Back when he ran away from a funeral he didn't want to happen, but couldn't stop? Maybe Dad was still running? Maybe leaving for my dad was like starting fires for me—things we couldn't control, turning into actions we shouldn't do. If that was true, then maybe when Dad went out of town he wasn't leaving me but only running away from the memory of my mother's death. Maybe.

A warm breeze swirled around me, lifted my hair like a hand running through it. The beginning of a smile formed on my lips as I picked up a rock and placed it in an open space to mark the trail I was on.

The trail continued along the side of the mountain. The air grew cooler even as the breeze died away. Every so often I squinted against the sun as I tried to see the mountain's top, but all I could see were pines rising into the sky. The pines' shadows stretched out over the trail. The day was slipping away. Ever since I'd left the cave, my stomach had been closing into a fist, and as I watched the sun sink lower, that fist tightened.

I took off Aitatxi's beret and held it to my face. The worn fabric felt like beard stubble against my cheek. I smelled dust and wine and sheep on the beret. Aitatxi was everywhere. I closed my eyes, and when I opened them, I looked up to see above the pines the top of an oak.

"*Harrapatu aritz ona,*" my father had written on the cave wall. I'd found the good oak.

I put the beret back on and was about to tell Mikelats to get the flock going faster when the sheep came to a stop. I moved up through them to where Mikelats sat at the base of the last part of the trail. Just like on the map, the trail rose sharply for about two hundred feet, and at its end sat the biggest oak tree I'd ever seen. The limbs of the tree were twisted and spread out like green fireworks frozen at the moment of explosion. The oak in the farm's pasture was over forty feet tall with a trunk as wide as my outstretched arms. It would have taken at least two of the farm's trees to make this *aritz ona.* The tree looked exactly like the one Dad had drawn on the wall. The *etxola* would be there.

I'd made it.

Well, almost. Something the map didn't show was that nearly half of the trail was washed away by rain. The crumpled outer edge fell straight down. The remaining trail was only about three feet wide. I gazed at the jagged rocks far below and stepped back, dizzy. I steadied myself against the mountainside.

"Dad?" I called up toward the *etxola,* but got no answer. He wasn't there.

I turned back to the flock. A lot of the sheep were lying down on the trail. Others had their tongues hanging out. The fist in my stomach clenched. I was going to have to take the sheep up the trail one at a time. And, even with my help, I wasn't sure some of them could make it.

I'd come so far only to have the stupid trail be washed away. My jaw jutted forward and the old anger started to build. But before it ignited, I grabbed the nearest sheep around the middle and with a grunt lifted it off the ground. I hugged the bleating sheep to my chest, and with its legs dangling down between my own, I started up the trail.

I didn't get more than a few feet with the sheep's face pressed up against mine before my arms started burning. The sheep struggled to get loose, and before we both fell over the edge, I set the sheep down in front of me. I kept a two-fisted grip on its wool as rocks clattered down the mountainside. I tried not to listen to how long it took for them to hit the bottom. I was scared enough as it was. Mikelats barked behind me.

"*Isilik,*" I said, working myself forward as I carefully shuffled the sheep up the trail.

When I got to the top, I found a gap where the last five feet of the trail were completely washed away. The opening fell down into nothing. There was no way the sheep and I were going to make it across together. On the other side of the opening, grass sloped up to the base of the oak. Beyond that I saw part of a wooden corral and the roof of what must be the *etxola.* I was so close. My body tingled. All that was left was for me to jump over the missing piece of trail. Only there was a flock of sheep I needed to think about.

I was trying to figure the best way to throw the sheep over the gap when the sheep wiggled free from my grip and jumped across onto the grassy slope.

"You're welcome," I said and then called back to Mikelats, who ran up the trail as if it were level ground and leaped across the gap.

"Showoff," I said, then added, "*Gelditu*—stay, Mikelats."

I started down the trail. Only thirteen stinking sheep to go.

As I brought the next sheep up the trail, I tried to sing a song, but I couldn't get a melody into my head; there was no room. I needed to focus on each step I took. One wrong foot and bye-bye sheep and bye-bye me. Right then, I wished I was a true *artzaina,* like Oxea, and could walk up the trail with a sheep under each arm. But no, for me it seemed it would always be the hard way, one step at a time. When I got up to the top, the second sheep backed away from the gap and pushed up against my legs.

"*Joan,*" I said, and thought about giving the sheep a kick

in the rear to get it going. But instead I callled to Mikelats. The dog jumped back over to my side of the trail and then nipped at the sheep's heels. That was all it took. With a loud "*baa*" the sheep jumped onto the pasture. Mikelats snorted as if to say, "Was that so hard?"

"*Mil esker,* Mikelats," I said and started down the trail for the next sheep.

I got the next few sheep up with no problem, but then it was Rollo's turn. Rollo was so fat that he barely fit on the trail. Twice he sent loose rocks over the trail's edge. And each time I held my breath as I listened to the rocks bounce against the side of the mountain. I was sure there was no way even Mikelats' nipping could get Rollo over the gap. But when we got to the top of the trail, Rollo gave a short run and jumped to the far side with no trouble. I shook my head. You could never tell about sheep.

By the time I got the last sheep to the top, the day was gone. The moon was rising, and in its pale light I could just make out my footprints mixed with those of the sheep's hooves trailing back down the trail. Further below that, the trail hugged the side of the mountain as it disappeared into the pines. The world beyond was covered in darkness. Dad was hidden in that darkness. I wanted some way to let him know I was all right. So I leaned my head back and let out my *irrintzina.* My cry unfurled in the air as it sank into the trees below. I didn't really expect Dad to hear my call, but I felt better for having let it out. So I gave a second *irrintzina,* and to my surprise, my call was answered.

Dad? I held my breath and listened. He was calling back to me. But then what I thought was Dad's *irrintzina* continued to rise and changed into the drawn-out howl of a coyote. I shivered even as I wiped sweat from the side of my neck. I needed to get the sheep in the corral and start a fire to keep the coyotes away. But when I turned to jump over the gap, I heard a "*baa*" from below. I'd forgotten one of the sheep.

No, I remembered bringing up the last one. There were no more sheep down there. Then I heard the "*baa*" again, and recognized its sad sound.

"Gaixua?"

Keeping my hands on the side of the mountain, I used my feet to feel my way down the now dark trail. How had Gaixua made it alone through the wilderness? How had he escaped being killed by the coyotes? I slid one foot forward at a time. Maybe because Gaixua was so small, he'd gone unseen. But no, coyotes didn't need to see a sheep to find him—Gaixua's smell would have given him away.

A coyote howled again.

"Deabrua's kids," I said as I reached the bottom of the trail to find a trembling Gaixua. I knelt down and hugged the sheep. "I thought you were dead."

Gaixua nuzzled me with his wet nose.

"Stupid sheep," I said, and was glad no one from school could see me. Not that I cared at that moment what wise-crack Rich would make. I was just happy that Gaixua was alive.

Then I saw a dark figure on the trail behind Gaixua. I scrambled to my feet as what I thought was a coyote barked. Mikelats? How had the dog gotten to the bottom of the trail without my noticing him? But as the dog came forward, I knew without even seeing whether his tail was up or down that it was Atarrabi.

"Atarrabi, you came."

The dog licked my outstretched hand. That was how Gaixua had made it. He wasn't alone, Atarrabi was with him.

But before I could even finish the smile growing on my face, another coyote howled.

"*Guazen,*" I said as Gaixua pushed against my knees, and we started up the trail.

The next howl was closer and made the skin of my face tighten. I smelled something that reminded me of an unwashed dog—only dirtier and wilder. The coyote howled again. He was nearby. I stared into the night, afraid of what I might see. But the trail was empty. Still, Atarrabi growled.

We were about halfway to the top when, through the sweat that burned my eyes, I saw something shift in the darkness ahead. There was a coyote on the trail in front of me. The sheep up top began to bleat in fear.

"*Zaza urrun,*" I yelled. "Go away." But I knew that while he heard me, the coyote wouldn't listen. I let go of my hold on Gaixua's wool to wipe the sweat out of my eyes. And when I did, Giaxua bolted from between my legs and ran up the trail. Atarrabi chased after him.

Unbalanced, I fell backward onto the rocky ground. There was a snarling. Atarrabi yelped.

"Mikelats, Atarrabi, *heldu niz*—I'm coming."

I scrambled to my feet and sprinted forward. In my hurry, I forgot about the gap in the trail and almost fell headlong into the dark opening. Unable to stop, I jumped.

Where the far side should have been, my foot found only air. Then the edge of the trail slammed up under my armpits. My chin shot forward and hit stone. A flash of light went off in my head. I dug my fingers into the dirt and tried to pull myself up.

My eyes were watering from the blow to my chin. I felt my own hot breath on my face. I struggled for a foothold, but my feet slid against the smooth side of the mountain. There was a buzzing like static on a radio in my head. And through the static I heard Aitatxi singing, "*Erten al daugut, bizia besala, mendia behar pastu, urratz bat aldian . . .*" His voice grew fainter as if the radio were losing power.

I couldn't hold on. I was going to fall. I looked up into the sky full of stars. All my ancestors from the first *Eskualduna* in Eden were watching me from above. I was sorry. I had failed.

Then, even as my grip loosened, I was surrounded by the smell of wet wool and sour wine. Strong arms closed around me, and something that felt like gravel dragged against my skin. The Mamu's *irrintzina* filled the air. He was Aitatxi and Oxea and their father and his father and his, back until before there were words. Back when we only had our *irrintzinak.*

And as the Mamu's *irrintzina* rose, so did I.

twenty-two | hogeibi

School ended and summer began while I was in the hospital. Ms. Helm's class and the whole seventh grade sent me a get well card. Rich wrote, "*Esawn owncha,* Buddy" at the bottom.

The day I got out of the hospital, Dad and I drove to the farm to check on the sheep. Dad bought the sheep back from the Outwest Dude Ranch, paying for all the original thirty-two, in order to avoid any legal problems.

"This came for you," Dad said as housing developments dissolved into fields of cotton. He handed me an envelope with long, loopy writing. The postmark said Ohio. Inside, I found a note from Connie: "Thought you might like a memory from your outlaw days," along with a picture of me and Aitatxi.

It was the one she took of us on the golf course. We are both wearing berets. I look young, like a little kid, and Aitatxi, well, he looks like Aitatxi. He is grinning, and I remembered how he pulled me to his side and said, "*Zuretako hauda*—this is for you." I also remembered how I pulled away from him. But the picture doesn't show that. It was taken before then, while I'm still leaning into Aitatxi, with my hand on his coat, holding on to him.

I put the picture back in the envelope and tucked it into my shirt pocket. Then, even though my jaw ached from the hairline fracture I had, I said, "When we get to the farm, can you show me how to play *pelote?*"

"*Pelote?* Now, then, what made you think of that?"

"The first time Aitatxi spoke to Amatxi was at a *pelote* match."

"I didn't know that," Dad said. "But we don't have a ball."

"I bet Aitatxi has one of your old balls at the farm."

"You're probably right," Dad said. "Okay, just as long as you don't overdo it, Matt."

"Matt?" I said. "I'm no bat. My name is Mathieu."

Dad chuckled. "Mathieu it is."

When we reached the farm, I found a ball in the hall closet under a stack of *zakuas* and a jai alai basket. I gave the ball to Dad, who bounced it twice on the wooden floor, squeezed it tight in his right hand, and said, "*Guazen,* Mathieu."

I followed him out to the barn.

"Now, then." Dad stood in the dirt facing the side of the barn. "You don't have to see the ball as much as feel where it's going."

The sheep watched us from their pen as Dad showed me how to use my hand to bang the ball against the barn wall. My jaw throbbed with pain every time I hit the ball with my open hand, but I kept playing. When I missed a shot, Atarrabi and Mikelats ran and got the ball, and we started again. While we played, I asked Dad to tell me about how he met my mother. And even though the words my father used were different from Aitatxi's, the story was the same and ended with me.

My father and I played *pelote* until it grew dark, and still we played. The bang of the ball against the wood fell into rhythm with the beating of my *bihotza.* I played with sweat in my eyes and the sound of my father's hard breathing in my ears. And when we were done, Dad and I took off our shirts and sat with our bare backs against the barn. The warm summer air was cool on our wet skin, and even though it hurt my jaw I told Dad all the things me and Aitatxi did—about stealing the sheep and the rain and the coyotes and how the Mamu saved me.

When I was through with my story, Dad smiled and told me that the Mamu was make-believe. That I was the one who penned up the sheep and made the fire that kept the coyotes away until morning when Dad remembered about the other *etxola* and arrived with the police to find me asleep with the dogs curled up on either side of me.

"There was no Mamu, Mathieu," Dad said. "Only you."

But I know better.

"Now, then, I've been thinking," Dad said. "What would you say to us moving back out to the farm?"

I leaned over to my father and whispered in his ear, "That wouldn't suck."

Dad laughed and ran a hand through my hair. I knew then that I was home.